PACIFIC SHORES
- BOOK 1 -

Beyond the Waves

PACIFIC SHORES
- BOOK 1 -

Beyond the Waves

Brynn STEWART

PACIFIC SHORES SERIES

Contemporary Christian Romance

Beyond the Waves – BOOK ONE

Caught in the Current – BOOK TWO

Song of the Surf – BOOK THREE

Written in the Sand – BOOK FOUR

Other books by Brynn Stewart

THE RIVERSONG SERIES

Contemporary Christian Romance

Angel Kisses and Riversong – BOOK ONE

Soft Kisses and Birdsong – BOOK TWO

Butterfly Kisses and Windsong – BOOK THREE

HEARTS OF HOLLYWOOD

Contemporary Christian Romance Novellas

My Blue Havyn – BOOK ONE

Mistletoe and Mochas – BOOK TWO

Kittens and Snow Flurries – BOOK THREE

MISTY COVE

Contemporary Christian Romance Novellas

The Heart of Christmas – BOOK ONE

The Wonder of Christmas – BOOK TWO

Beyond the Waves
PACIFIC SHORES, Book 1

Cover design by Lynnette Bonner of Indie Cover Design
images ©
www.depositphotos.com, File: #112933428 - couple
www.depositphotos.com, File: #31945117 - waves

Author photo © Emily Hinderman, EMH Photography

ISBN: 978-1-942982-54-8

Beyond the Waves is a work of fiction. References to real people, events, establishments, organizations, or locales are intended only to provide a sense of authenticity and are used fictitiously. All other characters, incidents, and dialogue are drawn from the author's imagination.

Printed in the U.S.A.

Philippians 3:13 & 14

But one thing I do: Forgetting what is
behind and straining toward what is ahead,
I press on toward the goal to win the prize for
which God has called me heavenward
in Christ Jesus.

Chapter 1

Taysia blinked away tears as she keyed in the digits to the security panel at the front door of Mom's Gym. Her bag, slung over one shoulder, whispered against the slick nylon of her sweat suit as she hurried down the back hallway toward her office. The last thing she needed right now was to bump into Marie.

Pushing open her office door, she paused to absorb the peace of her little domain. The scent of new carpet and fresh paint assailed her. She liked the effect of her remodel. The dark green pile and mint-colored paint gave the room a cool, soothing feel that was heightened by the Thomas Kincade prints. She closed her eyes and inhaled the quiet, then forced the tension in her shoulders to ease on a long exhale of air.

Her fingers filtered across the top of the maidenhair fern on the stand to her right. This was where she lived and breathed. Well, here and the amazing beach at the edge of town, which was where she headed whenever she got the chance. There weren't many places more beautiful than the Oregon coast. But when she had to be inside, she needed the soothing coolness of this room to escape from her hectic schedule.

She stepped farther into the office and pushed the door shut behind her as her shoulders drooped a little. Today the living and breathing would come with more pain than usual.

She squeezed the base of her neck and rolled her head from side to side, trying to ease the low throb of a headache that had been threatening since the night before. Daddy hadn't shown up for their Friday dinner date last night, and when she'd gone to his house to make sure he was fine, it became obvious he'd forgotten all about it—not unusual these days.

With another sigh she set her bag down. She hated to admit it, but the signs of his decreasing mental faculties could no longer be ignored. She would have to make a decision soon.

Lord, I can't stand to see Daddy go downhill like this. Please just bring him back. Only a few months ago, he was just fine. This has all happened so quickly. I don't know what to do for him, Lord. Help me—

The buzz of the intercom interrupted her prayer. She stripped off her sweat-suit jacket as she moved toward the desk.

She punched the intercom button. "Yes?"

"Taysia? Is that you?"

Taysia rolled her eyes. *No, Marie, it's Billy Blanks, Tae Bo instructor extraordinaire.* Really, Marie could be denser than coastal fog sometimes.

"Yes, Marie, it's me. What?" She fired the words with the speed of a bullet, determined to end this conversation quickly. She loved Marie, but right now she didn't feel like talking to anybody, much less Queen Featherbrain. She angled her eyes toward the ceiling. *Forgive me?*

"*He's* here!"

Taysia pinched the bridge of her nose. With her seventeen-year-old receptionist, *he* could be any one of half a dozen men... Ever since Reece Cahill had broken up with the girl, she'd been on a bit of a boy binge, trying to soothe her hurting heart. Reece was a very nice guy, and Taysia doubted he knew just how badly he'd hurt Marie. But, sad to say, Taysia hadn't been surprised when she'd heard he'd broken things off. He'd always been more mature than Marie. Truth be told, he was more spiritually on track too. But Taysia was working with Marie on that, and she'd come a long ways from the broken, rebellious teen who'd walked in looking for work a year ago after her father, and only remaining parent in the home, had been sentenced to ten years for a B&E with intent to harm.

Yes, Marie had come a long way. Now, if only

they could get her past this boy-crazy stage.

The box boy at the local supermarket had been Marie's love interest *last* week.

This week Marie had been on the new-cop-in-town-pulled-me-over-just-for-running-a-stop-sign kick...

The conversation she'd had with Marie just yesterday rang through Taysia's head. Marie had giggled and chomped a large wad of bubble gum as she proclaimed, "After all, cops in Marinville just don't pull people over like that, especially not for running stop signs, so he must have wanted to meet me, right? You should have seen him, Taysia. He's so *gorgeous*!"

Taysia hadn't bothered to mention that in the small burg of Marinville, no one but Marie probably ever drove over the speed limit, much less ran a stop sign. The poor guy had most likely been bored out of his gourd and looking for any excuse to do his job.

Although, if he *had* gotten a look at Marie, he might *have* pulled her over just to meet her. To say Marie was beautiful would be an understatement. She was a petite brunette with big blue eyes that could swallow a man whole, and she knew how to use them to her best advantage. Taysia had seen her weasel her way out of more than one sticky situation by coquettishly angling her baby blues in the direction of an unsuspecting male. The new officer in town must have a heart of stone if he could look Marie in the eye and still hand her a ticket.

Yes, Marie was definitely beautiful; she was just missing a few boxes in the attic.

Oh, Taysia! Stop it! All she needs to do is grow up a little. Marie is a wonderful woman. She is a wonderful receptionist. When she's not—okay, enough!

Taysia pressed the intercom, wondering which male on planet Earth Marie was referring to this time. "Who, Marie?"

"*Him*! The new cop I was telling you about." She lowered her voice so Taysia barely heard what she said next. "And he's even more gorgeous than I first thought!"

"That's nice. Did you tell him this gym is geared toward pregnant women and new mothers with post-pregnancy flab on their bellies and thighs? Unless his name is Arnold and he's just delivered Junior, he should probably try Goddfry's down on Second."

A giggle crackled from the speaker. "He's not here to work out, silly. Wait...who's Arnold?"

Great. Now her love of obscure movies was showing. "Never mind."

"Whatever...anyway, he's here to see you."

The headache that had begun last night after her conversation with Daddy flared to life with a painful vengeance. She reached into her top drawer and snatched up the bottle of painkillers. *Sophia Clinesmith*. This had to be about her.

"Fine," she said into the speaker, "send him on back." Pouring three of the white pills into her palm, she tossed them to the back of her throat, swallowing them down with a swig from the ever-present water bottle on her desk.

Sophia Clinesmith.

The pain in her head sank its claws into her frontal lobe and clenched its fists. She rubbed at her brow and hoped those little pills would kick in sometime soon.

This visit was undoubtedly about the lawsuit. Taysia had known Sophia since elementary school. All her life Sophia had been gorgeous, willowy, blonde, and bratty. Sadly for Mom's Gym, she was also a model and had twisted her ankle on a pop can someone left in the gym's parking lot.

The injury wasn't severe, but Sophia had missed a fashion show because of it and had informed Taysia in no uncertain terms that she would be taking her case before a judge.

Some people never change.

Not long after, a mousy lawyer had shown up with some official-looking papers and told her an investigator would stop by in a couple of days to ask her some questions.

This must be her lucky day. *He's working on a Saturday?*

Taysia bent down, unzipped the cuffs of her powder-blue sweatpants, and slipped them off over her Nikes. She glanced at her watch. This cop could have five minutes of her time and not a minute more, or he would make her late for class. She smoothed her navy shorts and straightened her socks so she would be ready to go the minute she was able. Rummaging in her sports bag, she found a scrunchie and pulled her sun-bleached blonde hair back into a ponytail just as she heard the knock on her door.

She sat down behind her desk and picked up her water bottle. "Come in," she called as she took a sip. *I hope those painkillers will kick in sometime this year!* Maybe more water would help. She tipped the bottle up for a long swig, eyeing the door as she did so.

The officer pushed open the door and stepped into the room.

Taysia's eyes widened and she gave a startled grunt, spewing water everywhere. She clapped a hand to her mouth, attempting to stop the leak in the dam. It didn't work. The water trickled through her fingers and dribbled down the front of her dark green T-shirt, leaving ugly wet splotches. Still choking from shock, Taysia tried to swallow the measly few drops that remained in her mouth and regain some of her composure. Unfortunately, she drew in what was meant to be a calming breath at the exact moment she swallowed, which sent her into a gale of hacking coughs that would have done justice to an elephant with pneumonia.

And all the while Kylen Sumner stood in the

doorway with a smug smile, eyeing her as though she were a freak sideshow at the circus, hands resting on slim hips, one black eyebrow cocked. “Hello, Taysia. Glad to see me back home, I see.”

Taysia set down her water bottle with a thunk and looked around the room for a means of escape. With two strides she was at the door to her private bathroom, snatching up her gym bag on the way in. She needed to find a towel—and her composure. “I’ll be right back,” she tossed over her shoulder. “Have a seat.”

She heard him mutter, “Kylen! How long have you been home? It’s so nice to see you again!”

Hah! Fat chance! If that was the greeting he’d expected to receive, he had certainly gotten the surprise of his life, hadn’t he?

The thought cheered her a little, but she still shut the door with a little too much oomph. The vibration shook the walls and sent her toothbrush holder clattering into the sink with a loud commotion. She snatched it up quickly to stop the noise and eyed the door for a moment, half-expecting Kylen to burst in to see if she was alright. Setting the ceramic holder back into place, she leaned her fists into the counter and stared at her face in the mirror.

Her cheeks could rival a stoplight for color, and her heart was thundering like a dryer full of tumbling tennis shoes.

Who would have thought that the mere sight of one man could rattle her so? But then again, this wasn't just any man. This was Kylen Sumner. *Helga's high heels!* The memories he brought back. And like the man, these weren't just any memories. These were Kylen Sumner memories—not happy-go-lucky-summer-day memories, although there were those, but unpopular, Fatty-Four-Eyes, nerd-of-the-decade memories. Memories she'd just as soon forget.

She blinked and focused on her image in the mirror. She would not let him back into her life.

Not again.

Not ever!

Kylen bolted upright in his chair as Taysia burst out of the bathroom. She had changed into a light-blue T-shirt that brought out the blue gray of her eyes.

She met his gaze only briefly. "Wish I could stay and chat about old times, but I'm late for a class as it is." She brushed by him and headed for the door, her athletic gait sure and smooth. Slender, tan legs—

He swallowed and forced his attention to the floor, staring at a white speck of fuzz on the green carpet.

"Taysia, someone else is going to have to cover your class. I'm here about Sophia." His tone was all business, but he eyed her speculatively, knowing that the history between the three of them was not making this situation any easier.

"Fine. Yes, I know. She's suing me over a pop can in the parking lot. Really, you'll have to catch me another time." She opened the door and gestured for him to leave.

"She's not suing you anymore—maybe. I talked her into trying to settle through mediation."

She gave him a disbelieving glare. "You're serious?"

"As a heart attack." He stood. "But we have some things to talk over, so, please, you need to cancel your class."

Taysia sighed and moved to her desk. "There's such a thing as an appointment, you know. You couldn't have called ahead and found a time when I was free?"

"And missed the look on your face when I walked into your office?"

The glare she slanted his way would have melted plastic.

Realizing he probably shouldn't have brought that up, Kylen held up both hands. "She said she would like to settle in mediation and hopes you'll agree. Otherwise she's going to follow through all the way to court."

Taysia sighed and reached a hand to the muscles at the base of her neck. "Who does she want to mediate this?"

Kylen shoved his hands deep into his pockets and cocked one eyebrow, giving what he hoped was an "I'm innocent" shrug.

"You?"

He nodded.

Taysia sank mechanically into her desk chair. "Fine. I'll cancel the class." He watched as she placed her index finger in her mouth and nibbled on the outside cuticle, her thumb resting under her chin. She only did that when she was nervous or overwhelmed. She made no move to call her receptionist.

Coming around to her side, he asked, "Your receptionist, what's her name?"

"You gave her a ticket."

His brow knitted in a frown. Where had that comment come from? He thought back. Yes, he had given the girl a ticket last week for...something. Her name escaped him. "What's her name?"

"Marie."

He pressed the intercom. "Marie?"

"Yes. Who's this?"

"This is Officer Sumner. Listen, something's come up. Layne—uh, Miss Green—isn't going to be able to make it to her class. She would like you to cancel it, all right?" Kylen let up on the button.

Marie's cheery voice buzzed over the speakers. "You got it!" Too cheery. Her words vibrated with the triumphant timbre of a gossip who'd just overheard the juiciest tidbit of the decade. Kylen suppressed a groan. *Great*. The last thing he wanted was to start rumors about Layne, again.

Turning to face Taysia, Kylen relaxed back onto the desk, stretching his legs out. “So...you want to head down to Joe’s Ice Cream Truck for old times’ sake?”

She glared daggers at him and jabbed the intercom. “Marie?”

He knew her irate frown originated in the past.

“Yes?” Marie’s voice crackled.

Taysia glanced down at the intercom, her face suddenly drooping wearily. “Could you lead First Trimester Fitness today? All the gals in there know the routine fairly well. Just make sure not to push them too hard. And don’t forget to open the class in prayer and read Psalm 139. I’ll be done here in half an hour, so I’ll be able to lead Second Trimester Stretches.”

“Sure, I can do that.” The girl sounded a trifle unsure, but he gave her props for willingness to help Taysia out.

Kylen sighed. The past was the past, but how he wished he’d handled things differently. He crossed his arms to keep himself from reaching out to touch the softness of her cheek. She looked tired. Really tired. “I’m sorry, Layne. You’re right. I should have called and found out when you were free.” He didn’t add that he’d been afraid she would tell him to take a long midnight hike on a short cliff-side trail.

“Yes, you should—” She waved a hand. “Don’t worry about it.” Her face softened a little.

He needed to lighten the mood. "Just be glad I am free today, and that she agreed to allow me to mediate." He gave a magnanimous grin. "I could be here to arrest you, drag you down to the jail, and lock you up for life without parole! You low-down, parking-lot-full-of-pop-cans piece of scum, you."

She rolled her eyes and buried her face in her hands, but not before he saw the corner of her mouth quirk in response. Shoulders slumping, she asked, "So? What does she want?"

"She's claiming you cost her a multimillion-dollar contract."

"What!?" Her head snapped up.

He shrugged. "Apparently there was some bigwig scout-type guy at the show she missed because of her ankle. He signed on one of the other models to work for him, and Sophia is claiming you cost her that job." He paused, then grinned. "That's what she's *claiming,* but I don't think she really believes it."

Taysia sighed. "Why are you here, Kylen?"

His heart kicked into double-time rhythm. Standing, he sauntered over to look out her office window. A light breeze danced through the leaves of a tree just outside. Past a couple buildings, he caught a glimpse of the azure-blue ocean. Finally he made himself speak around the lump in his throat. "You know why I'm here, I just told you. Sophia—"

"Not *here* here. *Home* here."

He turned, studying her face intently. Did he dare tell her? Would she believe him if he told her she hadn't been far from his thoughts for the past five years? That he'd been as shallow as they came during high school, and he hoped one day she'd be able to forgive him? That he thought he just might be in love with her?

Now's as good a time as any.

"I came home because...I got a job offer." *Wimp!*

She huffed and waved a hand in his direction. "Fine. Whatever. It's a free country." She worked her lower lip with her teeth. "I just...I can't believe you're here. When did you move back home?"

Kylen winced inwardly at her stark misery, but was careful to keep his face bland. He had invaded her safe haven. Brought back all the painful memories. *God, help me to make up for the past. Help her to see I'm changed. Trustworthy.*

"I just got here the middle of last week. I'm living next door to you, in my parents' basement apartment. They are on a long vacation in Australia, so it worked out great for me to stay there while they're away."

Her face blanched. "Please, just..." She motioned toward the door. "Go. I can't...I can't do this right now."

It was the dejection and the desire in her voice that pushed aside his earlier resolve to keep his hands to himself. Kylen stepped toward her, intending to wrap her in a comforting embrace, but at the first touch of his fingers on her shoulders, she shoved back in her office chair, launching out of reach. Stark panic covered her face as though she had just come perilously close to falling off the edge of a cliff.

"Don't you touch me, Kylen Sumner!" She held out a trembling finger in his direction. "Don't you dare touch me."

"Layne—"

"And stop calling me Layne! You're the only one who ever used my middle name, and I don't want...you don't have the right..." She pressed her lips together tightly and shook her head. "Just don't call me Layne."

His shoulders sagged. What was the use? How many times had he regretted his actions? How many times had he thought about calling her? Dreamed about her? Wished she could forgive him? He rubbed his cheek, his day-old stubble rasping under his fingers. "I told you on the beach that day—" His words cut off as he stared into her eyes, willing her to believe him. His gaze never wavered and he held his breath, waiting for her response.

For an intangible moment he thought her face softened, but with the speed of a shuttering camera lens, her expression hardened into an unreadable mask.

Kylen shut his eyes and pressed fingers and thumb to his brow, rubbing at the throb that pulsed there. This was not good. He looked up.

Taysia stood and moved to the window. The only sound that could be heard was the soft song of a bird in the tree outside. She turned toward him and studied him boldly with large, serious eyes.

"Kylen, there is one thing good that came from our relationship. After that day on the beach, I really thought about what you said. You seemed"—she hunched her shoulders—"different. So I looked into it, and found it made sense. Jesus was what I had been searching for my whole life. I had made some really big mistakes, you know?" She blushed, clearing her throat. "And at that point in my life I was wondering, 'What's the purpose of going on?' Because of what you said that day on the beach, I gave my life to Christ and my mother gave her life to the Lord, as well, before she died." She smiled a sad smile, tears glimmering in her eyes at the mention of her mother. "I'm still praying for Dad, but one of these days..."

Kylen spoke huskily. "That's great, Lay—Taysia. I just wish things had been different before then, especially between us."

She shut her eyes, pressed her lips together, and spun back to the window. After a moment, she gave one nod. For a moment silence stretched, then she glanced over her shoulder and looked him in the eye. "I forgive you, Kylen."

He blinked slowly, forcing himself to breathe normally even as his heart soared.

Her gaze fixed once more on the scene outside the window as she continued. "I've known for a long time that I needed to find you and tell you, but I always put it off. You weren't entirely to blame. I was in the wrong, too. I could have made more of an effort to be your friend, and that night—"

"Taysia, don't."

She nodded. "Some things are better left in the past. How does that verse go? We forget what is behind and press on toward our goal, right?"

"And thank God for His grace and mercy."

"Yes," she whispered in a choked voice, blinking back tears.

The room was silent for several moments as he waited for her to compose herself. He moved so he could at least see the side of her face.

Forcing a professional tone, Kylen said, "So back to this lawsuit business. Do you have time to talk this over with me tonight?" A blush heated her cheek, and he eyed her speculatively.

She didn't answer right away, but when he continued to wait silently, she said, "No...I'm going to Blaine Pittman's for dinner."

Kylen's jaw hardened. "Blaine Pittman? Isn't he a little young for you?"

She snorted. "He was only a year behind us, Kylen." Shrugging, she lifted her chin. "Anyhow, I don't see how Blaine is any concern of yours."

His fists clenched as he shoved them into his pockets. His voice dropped to just above a whisper. "I came home for a reason, Layne."

She turned and met his gaze then, a question on her face.

"I came home because I'm in love with you."

A small strangled sound escaped her throat as she collapsed back against the windowsill.

Chapter 2

Marie Sinclair swallowed as she eyed the group of women before her. Taysia had never entrusted her with teaching a class before. But if she were honest, her nervousness didn't stem from the fact that this would be her first time teaching. She'd sat in on enough of these and helped Taysia demonstrate the stretches and exercises enough to know the routine down pat.

"If I can have your attention, please?" She gulped. Hopefully no one had detected the quaver in her voice.

As she waited for the class to quiet, she rubbed her thumb over the laminated sheet of verses from Psalm 139 that Taysia read before each of her classes. She could almost say them from memory now she'd heard them so many times.

When all eyes were on her, she continued. "Miss Green has had something come up and has asked me to lead the class for her." She offered the women a grin. “So what do you say we make this short and sweet and get you all on your way a little early today, huh? You all deserve a break!”

Several of the women cheered, and Marie gave a little bow in response. “First let me open with the psalm.” Her hand trembled as she glanced down at the words on the page. She gritted her teeth and firmed her grip. This was all Reece’s fault. If only he hadn’t—no. None of this was his fault. She smoothed one hand down the front of her T-shirt and took a quick, calming breath, then forced the words past the constriction in her throat. “From Psalm 139, verses thirteen to sixteen. ‘For you created my inmost being; you knit me together in my mother’s womb. I praise you because I am fearfully and wonderfully made; your works are wonderful, I know that full well. My frame was not hidden from you when I was made in the secret place, when I was woven together in the depths of the earth. Your eyes saw my unformed body; all the days ordained for me were written in your book before one of them came to be.’”

She looked up. Several of the women in the class had placed hands over their abdomens as though already cradling the children they longed for.

Cassie Graham in the front row had tears in her eyes and a smile on her face. “Isn’t it wonderful to know God had plans for each of us even before we came into being?”

Marie tapped the edge of the plastic against the podium and nodded with as much of a smile as she could muster.

Hold it together, Marie. You don't know anything yet, for sure. Just hold it together.

Taysia fled, quite literally, leaving Kylen standing in her office with a bewildered-puppy-dog expression. She hated herself for her cowardice, but she couldn't stand the pressure for even one more second.

She dashed past the classroom and into the lobby, darting glances over her shoulder like an escapee from a mugging.

Marie must have seen her through the window in the door, because she poked her head out of the classroom. Taysia could hear the cooldown music already playing. The clients knew the last part of that routine well enough by now to handle it on their own. She waved a frantic gesture at Marie. "Come here and don't let him find me!"

Marie cocked her head and scrutinized her.

Pressing a finger to her lips, Taysia lunged behind the front desk and jerked open the janitor's closet. The cleaning cart sat right there, the big yellow bucket full of damp mop leaving no room for her. She spun back to face the counter, her eyes flitting to the cubby underneath Marie's desk. Too small. Kylen was headed this way—she could see him exiting her office on the security monitor.

Panic swelled in her chest. She was crazy to even be thinking of hiding from him. Much less in a closet! But Kylen had already broken her heart twice. She wasn't about to let him do it a third time! And facing him after his crazy admission held about as much appeal as drizzling lemon juice over an open wound.

There was nowhere else to go. She would just have to squeeze in. She stepped into the big yellow bucket, balancing precariously on the damp, squishy mop. Marie's wide eyes were the last thing she saw before the door swung shut on its automatic hinge. Total darkness and the smell of musty mop and ammonia engulfed her.

She groaned softly and pressed her forehead to the door. *Oh Lord, why now? Blaine and I are just starting to date, and he's a really great, trustworthy guy. So, why did Kylen have to show up today? I just can't deal with this, especially not on top of the situation with Daddy.*

She laid her ear against the door and heard the soft squeak of Marie's chair as she apparently sank into it.

Taysia held her breath.

She could hear Kylen's footsteps now.

"Marie, is it?"

Taysia lifted her head and held her breath. Marie might just get some foolish romantic notion in her head and tell him she was in the closet.

"Yes, Officer. Can I help you?" Innocence dripped from Marie's words.

Taysia sighed in relief.

"Can you give Taysia a message for me? You'll see her again today, right?"

"Oh yes, I'm sure I'll see her. Miss Green never mops around. *Mopes!* She never mopes around. She'll get over your little lover's spat and be back to work just in time for her next class, I'm sure."

Taysia gritted her teeth. *Lover's spat, my eye.*

Kylen's voice was serious. "Tell her, I meant what I said."

Taysia tensed, and the cart under her mop bucket rolled back and bumped into the wall. Jerking her arms wide to catch her balance, she smacked some cans on the shelf next to her. The cans clattered to the floor.

"What was that?" Kylen exclaimed.

Great! Taysia winced and grunted in pain, clutching her hand. The cart began a full-blown jitterbug, and she reached for the solid steadiness of the door just as it jerked open.

"Oh!"

Kylen, Marie right behind him, stared wide-eyed, jaw slack.

Flapping her arms desperately trying to regain her balance, Taysia searched frantically for anything to grab onto but the broad expanse of Kylen's shoulders. She lurched for the lintel, but as her weight pitched forward, the cart jostled backward and her hands missed the mark.

"Ah!"

Her shins scraped painfully across the top of the mop bucket, and she landed like a gangly giraffe in Kylen's arms. He grunted and stepped back into Marie, who squawked like a startled duck. All three of them landed in a tangled sandwich on the floor.

The mop fell out of the bucket and *thonk*ed Taysia on the head with a resounding crack. "Ow!"

Kylen rolled up onto one elbow, kicking away the mop and pushing Taysia over onto her back. "Are you okay?"

Taysia nodded with gritted teeth, refusing to let the groan trapped in her throat escape. Her right shin felt like a cat had mistaken it for a scratching post. A big cat!

Behind Kylen, Marie snipped, "I'm fine, Officer. Don't you worry about me, now. You're just *lying on my legs*!"

Kylen's eyes widened and he scrambled to his feet. "Sorry, Marie. Here." He reached down to help her up.

Taysia took advantage of his distraction to hobble to her feet. Blood dripped down her right leg. It was her own fault. How did she get herself into these situations? She bent to examine the wound.

"Taysia Layne Green, you are the craziest

woman I've ever met!"

Taysia didn't reply. What was there to say? Kylen and her blithering-idiot alter ego had been well acquainted from the day his parents had moved in next door. She sighed and limped toward her office to find a Band-Aid. Or ten.

Kylen started to follow, and she stopped dead in her tracks. "Don't!" She couldn't look him in the eye. "Just..." She gestured him toward the outside doors and promptly turned in the direction of her office. As she hobbled down the hall, her mind skimmed back over the years to a long-ago day just before her freshman year...

It had been a beautiful, sunny day when she noticed the new family moving in next door.

Taysia had walked down her drive until she stood beneath the shade of the old weeping willow tree. She decided to stretch out before her run under its sheltering branches so she could openly watch the new neighbors as they unpacked their moving van. The hanging boughs obscured her nosy gawking a little, as did her sunglasses.

Leaning one arm against the trunk, she pulled one foot up toward her bottom, stretching out her right quad. She balanced precariously for a moment to push her sunglasses up on her nose.

Hmmm, they have some nice things, these people. Must have money. Why, that sideboard alone costs more than all the furniture in our house put together. That would explain why they were moving into the old Johnston mansion next door.

Taysia glanced back down the drive at their own house—a little two-bedroom that Mom had painted a very soft blue. They had eaten hot dogs and chili for months afterward because the painter had charged them an outlandish amount, but it had been worth it. Mom loved the way the blue set off the exquisite red of her prized rosebushes. Taysia smiled. She liked it too. They had a nice home, even though it was small. She looked again to the newcomers as she stretched out her left quad. Her parents' house was very small, indeed, compared to the place next door. In fact, in a bygone era, the little blue house—and the roses—had belonged to the gardener of the Johnston mansion.

Yes, whoever was moving into the mansion had plenty of money. Besides the movers there was a man and his wife, but no kids.

She sighed. It had been too much to hope for. It would have been nice if they'd had a daughter her age. But it didn't matter, because if they did have a daughter, she would have money, which in Marinville meant she would be popular, and therefore, definitely *not* in the same group of friends as chubby Taysia Layne Green.

Oh well, she was working on the chubby part, at least. She had dropped fifty pounds since this time last year.

She turned to jog toward the beach and collided with a firm, somewhat lanky form. She let loose a surprised squawk even as she bounced back like a tennis ball and fell onto her backside. Her sunglasses tumbled off and landed in the grass a few feet away.

He was the best-looking boy she had ever seen.

"Why are you staring at us?" the boy asked.

Mouth dry, Taysia gawked at him in dumbfounded silence. He had black, curly hair and eyes as dark as a moonless midnight. A diamond stud winked at her from the lobe of one ear, drawing her attention to his high, angular cheekbones. He wore designer shorts, and his dirt-smudged polo hung from his shoulders with kingly grace. *Definitely popular!* And he had spoken to her! Her mouth was no longer just dry. It was parched. Like a sea sponge in the middle of a desert during a drought. She continued to gawk, her mouth hanging open.

She stared at him for so long he finally gasped, "Oh, you can't see! I'm sorry. Here!" He plucked her dark glasses from where they'd landed and placed them carefully into her hands. "And here I thought—"

She blinked and refocused on his face, unable to help herself.

He frowned at her. "You can see!" he accused. "What are you looking at?" He brushed at the corners of his mouth as though searching for stuck-on food. When she still made no reply, he reached a hand down to her with a puzzled expression. "Here, let me help you up. Did I hurt you?"

It was the concern in his voice that finally snapped Taysia out of her stupor as she accepted his help and scrambled to her feet. "N-no. I-I'm f-fine. T-thanks." She dusted off the seat of her shorts, but still couldn't seem to break eye contact.

With a quizzical grunt, he rubbed the back of his neck, scrutinizing her as though he didn't quite believe she had all her cards stacked right. He held out a hand again. "I'm Kylen Sumner." With a nod of his head in the direction of the mansion, he added, "We just moved in next door."

Taking his hand, Taysia managed to stammer, "A-Anastaysia L-Layne Green." Her face bloomed with heat. Whenever in the world had she introduced herself to someone by her full name? She was an idiot!

He cocked his head, and a twinkle leapt into his gaze. For a moment she thought he was going to point out her idiocy, but then he shrugged and seemed content to move on to another topic. He glanced at her jogging shorts and Nike running shoes—the ones she had saved all year to buy—and asked, "Were you going somewhere?"

"Jogging." She congratulated herself for not stammering.

"Okay. I should go help unpack my stuff, so I'll catch you later...*Layne*." The twinkle was back in full force, and this time it was accompanied by a grin. But to her surprise, there was no animosity in the teasing. Just simple friendship.

Friendship! That was the problem. If he hadn't been so kind to her that first summer; if he hadn't so quickly become her best friend; if he hadn't kissed her under her mother's backyard grape arbor, life would have been just fine for Taysia, and her blithering-idiot alter ego would probably never have been seen again. But he had done all those things. And she had trusted him.

Taysia hissed in pain as she swabbed hydrogen peroxide on the scrape on her shin. "If I'd had a lick of sense, I'd have begged Mom and Dad to move to Siberia that very day." Pressing the last Band-Aid on, she glanced at her watch. "Great! I'm five minutes late for class!"

Kylen slumped into his car and scrubbed his hands through his hair. Leaning his head back on the headrest, he closed his eyes. "Well"—he grinned and shifted forward—"that went well."

He glanced in the rearview mirror. His hair stuck up in all directions. He smoothed it down, put the key in the ignition, and headed toward the station.

He wasn't due in to work today. He was supposed to spend the weekend unpacking, but he needed the distraction of work right now. He'd just go into the station and organize his office. He fleetingly thought of the two hours of sleep he'd gotten last night, and considered a nap, but decided against it. He probably wouldn't be able to sleep anyway, if last night was any indication. He'd tossed and turned all night knowing he would see Taysia this morning.

Turning right onto Fifth, he grinned, then laughed outright as he remembered the look on Taysia's face when he'd jerked open the closet door. "She is something else." He didn't know whether to be flattered that he drove her crazy enough to make her hide in a cleaning closet, or insulted that she'd rather dance with a mop than face him.

I should have called to let her know I was home.

Pulling into the station lot, he parked and

headed inside.

"Sumner!" police chief Tom Hansen barked as soon as he walked through the door, "I'm glad you're here. Get your uniform on! A woman was just found wandering the north end of Sunset Beach. She's been beaten up pretty badly, and their office is currently short an officer. I'm going to need you on this one."

Kylen's heart sank even as he moved to grab the spare uniform he always kept in his office. So much for organizing his office.

He sighed as he did up the last button. Uniform in place, he headed toward the debriefing room to find out more.

Taysia stepped into her living room later that evening and dropped her gym bag by the door. Stretching her back, she glanced at the old grandfather clock. Nine fifteen. Good, she still had time for a jog on the beach.

After a long evening of paperwork, her muscles ached for some good, brisk exercise. Still in the workout clothes from her last class, she stepped back out the door just as Blaine pulled into the drive.

She leaned against the rail of her porch, enjoying the scent of salty sea air as she waited for him.

"Hey, gorgeous." He bounded up the steps.

"How's the most beautiful girl in Oregon tonight?"

She grinned. "I don't know. Have you seen her?"

"I'm looking at her right now."

"Well, in that case, I'm fine. Sorry I had to cancel our dinner plans. I had a day you wouldn't believe, and at the last minute I remembered my accountant is coming on Monday and I had to get everything ready for her."

He shrugged. "I popped the salmon steaks into the freezer after you called me." He grimaced. "Frozen lasagna was such a letdown, since my mouth was already watering for barbequed salmon."

"I'm really sorry, Blaine."

"Well, now I have something to look forward to, because you are definitely going to have to make this up to me." He socked a friendly punch to her arm.

She smiled, trying to ignore the guilt marching through her chest. She could have made it to dinner if she'd really wanted to. But the truth was, after her fiasco of a morning, she just hadn't been up for an emotional evening of trying to determine her feelings for Blaine. "I was just headed out for a jog. Care to join me?"

He glanced down at his dress shoes and slid his hands into his slacks. "I'm not dressed for it. Besides"—he winced good-naturedly—"you'd leave me in the dust."

Her grin broadened. "Oh, come on! I was easy on you last time. We jogged nice and slow, remember?"

His eyes narrowed and he stepped closer, glowering down at her. "What I remember is gripping my knees and sucking air while you laughed about my red face."

She giggled. "It was really red."

"All right, woman!" He reached for her ribs.

She jumped back and grabbed his hands, laughing. "I keep telling you, you need to get into shape so you can join the youth group in the after-church basketball games. The kids would love to have the chance to beat their fearless leader in a game."

He sighed and turned to lean his forearms against the rail. "Yeah, I know. You're right. Sports are just not my thing, Taysia." He glanced at her out of the corner of his eye. "I'd much rather do math than jog any day."

Taysia gave a mock shudder. "To each his own. How is your mom?"

He sighed. "She's a little better. I talked to Dad today. He said she had her last chemo treatment this morning. So she should really start feeling better as far as the nausea goes in a couple of days."

"I'm glad. I've been praying for her."

He turned toward her, his face suddenly serious. "That means a lot to me, Taysia." He kept his eyes on her face, his expression changing subtly.

An uneasiness began in her stomach.

His gaze dropped to her mouth.

She stepped back quickly. "Well"—she purposely leaned down and began to stretch out her legs—"I better get going if I'm to get to bed at a decent hour tonight. We have the youth group bake sale tomorrow, don't forget."

"Yeah. I didn't forget." There was disappointment in his voice. "I need to get home, too. I have a Sunday school lesson to finish preparing for."

"Come on, I'll walk you to your car."

As they moved down her steps, Kylen pulled in next door. He drove his squad car into the garage and then stepped out, eyeing them quietly.

Blaine draped an arm around her shoulders, and her irritation sparked.

"Kylen, right?" Blaine asked.

Kylen nodded. "Blaine, good to see you again. It's been a while." He transferred his gaze to Taysia.

Blaine tightened his arm around her. She would have stepped away from his embrace, but didn't want to embarrass him in front of Kylen.

She looked up. "Good night, Blaine. I'll see you in the morning."

Blaine placed a kiss on her temple.

Full-blown anger threatened to burst forth in a blaze of glorious harangue, but Taysia merely folded her arms and looked at her tapping toe.

"G'night, Taysia." With a final squeeze and a meaningful glance in Kylen's direction, Blaine climbed into his car and backed out of the drive. Thick, awkward silence filtered across the night.

Kylen stepped over the narrow flower bed that separated her drive from his and walked toward her. Even in the moonlight, she saw his dark gaze take her in from head to toe and felt her cheeks flame. She hoped the darkness hid it. She hadn't bothered to shower after finishing her last class. She ran a hand over her hair, sure it must be escaping from her ponytail by now and wishing she'd at least taken time to run a comb through it. *Stop it, Taysia, you're here to jog, not win a beauty pageant.*

"You're not going jogging alone, are you?"

Was that anger she saw in his eyes? She nodded. "I'll only be a few minutes. Thirty at the most."

"Do you know how dangerous it is for a woman to jog alone at night?"

Taysia sighed. "Kylen, this is *Marinville*!"

He stepped toward her, his black eyes glittering fire, and Taysia swallowed. Yes. It was definitely anger she saw.

"Yes. Marinville." He turned his burning gaze on the road where Blaine had just disappeared before transferring it back to her. "Pittman was just going to let you go by yourself? What kind of an idiot is he?"

Taysia's anger flared as hot as his own. "Maybe

he just doesn't overreact like you do!"

He opened his mouth to respond, then snapped it shut. Swallowing, he rubbed one hand over the top of his head and down his neck. His voice was husky when he finally spoke. "I need you to promise me you won't go jogging by yourself. Especially at night."

Taysia resisted rolling her eyes. "Kylen, the most dangerous thing in town is Mrs. Murton's Pomeranian!"

"I know. Just..." He shoved his hands into his pockets. "I just got home from working a case where a woman was badly beaten. I see things in my line of work, Layne, that probably make me a little more cautious than normal, sure. But everyone thinks, 'It will never happen to me.'" He stepped closer and lowered his voice. "Please, just wait for me? I'll come with you."

She swallowed, unable to pull her eyes from his. When he looked at her like that, she could almost agree to anything.

He took another step closer. "It's so good to see you again, Layne. Why did I wait so long to come home?"

Reality seeped into her senses, and she took a slow step back. "Kylen, nothing can come from this. I..." She glanced down. Suddenly she couldn't look him in the eye or go on. Much as she knew she should tell him to take a hike, her double-crossing heart wouldn't let her form the words. She needed to clear her head. She could never think straight when he was around! She took another step away. "I'll just go for a quick run. I'll be home in less than thirty minutes, I promise." She hoped he couldn't hear the desperation in her tone.

"Did *anything* I just said spark even a hint of caution in you!? Use some common sense, for heaven's sake!" In one swift stride he grabbed her wrist, then turned, gently but firmly pulling her toward his house.

Taysia stumbled after him. She tripped over the flower bed, almost losing her footing. "Kylen! What in the world has gotten into you?" Her heart pounded in her throat. She had no intention of going into his house with him. She clearly remembered what had happened the last time she'd allowed him to draw her into his house. "Kylen, stop!" She tried to pull her wrist from his grip, but he just kept walking. "Ky, please." Nervousness edged her voice with a tremor.

He stopped and spun toward her so quickly her momentum pitched her against the solid strength of his chest before she could stop. She let out a surprised squeak and looked up into his face.

Hands on her upper arms, he set her aright, but didn't let her go. His thumbs stroked hot traces across the goose bumps on her skin, and his voice was hoarse when he spoke. "I can't stand the thought..." He cleared his throat, looked away, blinked, then glanced back down at her. "I can't stand the thought of something happening to you, Layne. And frankly, I'm too tired to argue with you. I'm running on about two hours' sleep from last night, and if you're not careful"—his eyes darted to her lips and back—"I might do something we'd both probably regret later." He paused, then with a small grin amended, "Well, my only regret would be that you wouldn't kiss me willingly. Not yet."

At the raw desire she saw in his eyes, Taysia's heart kicked into post-marathon speed, and she opened her mouth to protest.

Kylen let go of one arm and brushed his thumb across her lips, caressing them, and, to her dismay, studying them intently. Her knees weakened, and only the pressure of his hand on her arm kept her on her feet. "Layne, please...just"—a muscle bunched along his jaw, and he tore his eyes away to look at the ground—"be quiet and follow me."

Abruptly, he let her go and spun on his heel, clearly expecting her to follow.

Taysia stumbled back a step to catch her balance, swallowed convulsively, and only took a second to decide it was probably wise just to do as he asked this once. If she turned toward the beach, he would just come after her.

Like a meek puppy, she followed obediently in his footsteps.

Kylen's pulse hammered as he banged open the door to his basement apartment and motioned Taysia in ahead of him. He was glad she'd decided to give in to his request, because in his present state of exhaustion he wasn't sure what his reaction might have been had she refused to comply.

"I'll only be a minute, have a seat." He gestured in the general direction of the couch.

Boxes were still scattered everywhere, and he kicked one aside as he made his way into his room. Closing the door, he sank onto the edge of his bed and clutched his head, willing his heart rate to return to normal. The things that woman did to his heart could be enough to kill a man.

He unbuckled his holster and laid it on his nightstand, where his gun would be in easy reach in the night.

In an effort to get his mind off of Layne, he thought back over his day. The woman had been taken to the hospital, where he had interviewed her. Her face had been black and blue and so swollen she could barely respond to his questions. But thankfully she was going to be all right.

Still, even the thought of how he'd feel if anything similar ever happened to Taysia made him feel sick.

It was pretty cut and dried that the woman's boyfriend, who had been high at the time, had been the perp, but they hadn't been able to find him today. Kylen had helped as much as he could, but the lead on the investigation would come from the Sunset Beach office.

Wearily he began to unbutton his uniform. He wanted nothing more than to crawl into bed and not come out for ten hours, but the minute he'd pulled into the drive and seen Taysia, he'd known he would have to go jogging with her before he would be able to sleep.

He pulled on a pair of navy jogging shorts and a T-shirt, grabbed his tennis shoes and socks, and stepped back out into the living room. Sinking onto a box labeled "books," he pulled on his socks. He could feel Taysia studying him.

"You look tired, Ky. You don't have to do this."

He bit the inside of his lip, determined to ignore her and his jumping pulse. She hadn't called him that since the night he'd first kissed her under her mother's grape arbor. He distinctly remembered it. He had kissed her and then pulled away with a sheepish smile. Her arms around his neck, she had looked up at him and smiled softly. "I think I love you, Ky. But I still say things are going to be different when school starts." He had promised her they wouldn't and kissed her again. That was the one and only time he remembered her calling him Ky, and now she had done it twice in the last ten minutes.

Finished tying his shoes, he stood abruptly and gestured toward the door.

"Ky?" She stepped near, concern illuminating her face.

He chuckled softly, knowing good and well she wouldn't be calling him that if she knew what it made him want to do. He tapped her nose. "Come on. I'm man enough to stay awake for the next half hour and keep up with you to boot. So let's go."

She arched her brows. "You haven't stretched out yet."

Leaning a hand against the wall, he pulled one ankle up to stretch out his quad. "Ever the instructor, huh?"

She made a small sound of acknowledgment in her throat, and he glanced at her, noticing that her eyes were fixed on his legs, a blush shading her cheeks. He suppressed a grin, his heart soaring with renewed hope. Even if she did have something going with Pittman, she at least still found him attractive. That was a beginning.

She had stolen his heart on a long-ago summer's day, and he had broken hers on a cold, rainy night, but hopefully with a lot of work and a little of God's help, they could get all the scattered pieces back together again.

Chapter 3

Taysia woke with a start. It was still dark, and she lay there a moment. *What woke me?* She held her breath, willing herself to hear over the top of her thudding heart. *Could it be Kylen?* No. She shook her head.

The previous evening, she and Kylen had jogged in companionable silence, and when they had arrived back at her house, he'd told her good night with strict instructions to lock her doors. She had done as he asked, baked her cupcakes for tomorrow's bake sale, then slipped on her usual shorts and T-shirt and gone to bed. Kylen was sleeping soundly in his house next door, she felt sure, but...

A thud followed by a grunt of pain penetrated the silence.

She gasped softly. Someone was in the house! They had stumbled into a piece of furniture!

Suddenly wishing she owned a guard dog, Taysia fumbled for her bedside phone and pressed 9-1-1 with trembling fingers.

Another thud, and something shattered in the dining room. Taysia pressed back against her headboard, clutching the phone like a security blanket.

"9-1-1 emergency, how may I help you?"

"There is someone in my house," Taysia whispered, willing down the panic surging through her veins.

"All right, ma'am. I'll get a unit on their way to you right now. Do you think you are in immediate danger?"

"I don't know." She dared not raise her voice even a fraction above a whisper. She fixed her eyes on the dark, gaping shadow of her bedroom door, shuddering at the thought of someone stepping through it. Suddenly Kylen's earlier concerns didn't seem so ludicrous.

"Okay, ma'am, listen to me. Are you alone in the room you are calling from?"

"Yes." She pulled the covers up closer to her chin, then rolled her eyes. Like that would prevent her from being discovered by whatever fiend was creeping through her house.

"Do you have a place you could hide? Maybe someplace you could lock yourself into? Like a bathroom or a closet? If you do, I want you to take the phone with you and go there now."

Taysia eyed her parents' old armoire and tried to imagine opening its creaky old doors and climbing inside quietly. She shook her head. *No way*. The hinges on that thing groaned like a dam about to break. And the bathroom was two doors down the no-pinprick-of-light-to-be-found hallway. A tremor of fear slithered down her spine. There wasn't one thing that could entice her to step out there for even a second. She glanced at her bedroom's one window. Even if she could get the jam-prone wooden frame to open, she hadn't removed the storm windows yet. Blast this old house!

"No. No place to go."

"Okay, ma'am. Hang on. Our unit should be there shortly."

Suddenly Taysia remembered. "Kylen," she whispered. "He lives next door."

"I'm sorry, ma'am. Who?"

"Officer Sumner. He's my neighbor. Can you call him?"

Kylen groaned and rolled over, ignoring the phone. Two more rings and he flopped back and fumbled for the receiver.

"'Lo," he mumbled, squinting at his clock. Three twenty-eight.

"Officer Sumner?"

"Yes."

"This is Candy Bower from 9-1-1 dispatch. Your neighbor, ahh"—she paused, a keyboard clicking in the background—"Green, Anastaysia Green, is on the phone with us. She says there is an intruder on the premises and requested we call you."

Kylen came wide awake, lurched out of bed, and dropped the phone onto his nightstand. Grabbing his gun, he sprinted for his front door.

Barefoot and wearing only a pair of jogging shorts, he stepped out into the darkness, gripping his gun with both hands. He studied Taysia's house carefully. *Jesus, let her be okay. Please keep her safe.*

He ran toward the back of her house where her bedroom was. Pistol held at the ready, he pressed his shoulder against the siding at the corner and peered into her backyard. Empty. He slid along the wall, heading for the sliding door. Adrenaline pumped through his veins, and he tried to quiet his breathing. Feet planted next to her door, he quickly glanced into the room's interior, then jerked his head back. Everything looked still. He tried the door. It slid open easily, and he grimaced in frustration at Taysia's naïve irresponsibility. Quietly he pushed the door open farther and eased inside.

All was silent except for the crunch of something under his feet. Shards of pain pierced through him. He hissed a flinch, then gritted his teeth and moved on. There was no time for pain right now. He had to find Taysia.

He peered down the hallway. Nothing. Moving methodically, he cleared each room until he arrived at her bedroom. He stepped through the door. No one was there! His heart threatened to stop. "Layne?" He was surprised his voice sounded so steady.

With a soft gasp, Taysia leaped up from between her bed and the wall. "Oh, Ky!" She pressed a hand to her throat, moonlight reflecting off her tears as she rushed to him.

Holding his gun away at a safe angle, Kylen caught her to his chest with his free arm and kissed the top of her head. Looking toward heaven he rasped, "Thank You, God!" He blinked hard and rested his cheek on her hair. "Thank You!" He kissed her head again, and then with sudden swiftness, he put her from him. "Tell me what happened."

Taysia pressed a hand to her forehead. Her whole body trembled. "I don't know. I—I woke up and—and I heard a noise in the living room like someone stumbled into a piece of furniture and grunted. So—so I called 9-1-1 and asked them to send you over here. Then—then something broke. It sounded like"—her eyes widened—"my new crystal vase!" She started for the door, but he reached out and jerked her back. There were still a couple rooms he hadn't cleared on down the hall past her room.

"Keep talking."

"After I heard the glass break"—her teeth chattered and her head came up with a start, and her voice dropped till it was barely audible—

"whoever it was went into the bathroom, and I hid between the bed and the wall."

"You mean someone is still in your bathroom!? You should have said that first!"

Her eyes narrowed, and her hands clenched into fists by her sides. "Well, excuse me for being a little scatterbrained in the middle of the night when a person has just broken into my house!"

Just then they heard the toilet flush. Kylen blinked in disbelief. The perpetrator was flushing evidence! But of what?

Kylen motioned her to get down. "Stay here!" he whispered as he dashed into the hallway and flipped on the light.

Back pressed against the wall, gun held at the ready, he slid toward the bathroom. Taysia had ignored his command and crawled to her bedroom door. She poked her head out to peer down the hall. He started to motion for her to get back just as the bathroom door opened.

With a swift jerk, he leveled his gun. "Freeze!"

An old man stepping from the room halted so suddenly he almost lost his balance.

Eyes round as tennis balls, the man thrust gnarled hands straight up. The tips of his fingers rammed into the lintel above his head with a loud crack. "Ow!" His bulging eyes never left Kylen's gun as he scuttled a reluctant inch forward and again stiffened his arms, pinning his ears to his head.

"Taysia! I'm Taysia's father. Don't shoot.

Please. Don't! Shoot!"

Recognition hit Kylen at the same time as Taysia screeched, "Daddy! Kylen, it's Daddy! Don't shoot!"

Kylen lowered his gun, a release of breath easing his thundering pulse.

Mr. Green, arms still ramrod straight, looked from Kylen down to his gun, then glanced at Taysia and swallowed thickly. Slowly he lowered his arms, patted his chest, and ran a hand back over his disheveled white hair. He looked back at the gun. "I need to use the restroom again. Excuse me, please." Turning, he closed the bathroom door.

Kylen slumped against the wall and glanced at Taysia. She too had sagged in relief, forehead pressed to her knees.

The bathroom door had only been shut for three seconds when it jerked open and Mr. Green charged out like a bull that had just seen a red flag. "Young lady, what are you doing with that man in your bedroom?"

"Daddy!"

"Sir!"

Kylen wanted to laugh at the crazy turn of events, but instead he looked at Taysia, motioning for her to explain.

"Daddy, you remember Kylen Sumner—"

"Of course I remember him! He broke your heart! So what in thunderation are you doing with him in your bedroom?" He sized up Kylen's bare chest and legs with a glare of decided distaste.

Kylen ejected his mag and the remaining round. Weariness hit him in a wave, and he pressed his lips together grimly. He needed a moment to clear his head, and besides, the bottoms of his feet felt like they were on fire. He hobbled toward the dining room and a chair.

Taysia pressed one palm to her forehead, unable to believe what had just transpired. “Daddy! Please, just listen for a minute.” She tried to calm her father. “Kylen lives *next door*. I heard you in the living room and thought you were a robber or...something. I called 9-1-1, and they sent Officer Sumner over right away. He wasn’t sleeping here!” She shook her head. “Heavens, no!”

Kylen grunted from out in the dining room.

Taysia ignored him. She had probably hurt his feelings with her vehement denial. *Good, maybe he’ll get the picture!* “What in the world are you doing here anyway, Daddy?”

Daddy had the sense to at least look sheepish but didn’t answer the question.

Frustrated, Taysia glanced down. Bloody footprints marred the length of her hallway! She gasped. “What on earth?” She flipped on her bedroom light. They were in her bedroom too!

Her heart lurched and she rushed down the hall. "Kylen?"

"I'm in here. Careful when you come in here. There's glass everywhere. Get the light, would you?"

Taysia rushed toward the dining room and paused on the threshold as she flipped on the light. Her heart began a tympanic rhythm. She stared at the ground in horror. Shards of her new crystal vase winked and glistened like diamonds sprinkled across the floor. But it was the bloody footprints that set her heart to racing. *Kylen's* bloody footprints.

Kylen sat at the dining room table with one foot on a pile of paper napkins he'd spread on the floor while the other, resting on his knee, turned up at an odd angle as he blotted it. The napkin holder sat empty in the middle of the table next to his gun. He bent his head closer to his foot. "I think I'm going to need tweezers."

Taysia swallowed. Splinters of glass in his foot could not be good. "Daddy, could you please sweep this mess up while I help Ky get the glass out of his feet?"

She turned without waiting for an answer. In her bedroom she slipped on some flip-flops and then headed to the bathroom, where she gathered tweezers, hydrogen peroxide, Neosporin, and Band-Aids. Quickly, she headed back to the dining room, grabbing a roll of paper towels from the kitchen on the way.

"Here, let me," she said, taking the wad of napkins from Kylen and trying to ignore the long stretch of muscled leg attached to his foot. She couldn't let his good looks lure her into the trap of falling for him again.

She pulled out a chair and sat down, looking at her father, who was quietly sweeping. What in the world was Daddy doing in her house in the middle of the night? Was his mind that far gone? She pressed her lips together, fearing the answer.

She would have to talk to him about it later. Right now she needed to help Kylen.

"Why don't you just put your foot up on the table. I think I will be able to see better that way." She unscrewed the cap from the bottle of hydrogen peroxide.

"Whatever you say, Doc." Kylen rested one leg on the table's edge and clasped his hands behind his head.

Her attention snared on the well-defined bulge of his biceps. The muscular shoulders. The rigid six-pack of his abdomen. Her father cleared his throat, and heat infused her face. She met Kylen's quizzically amused glance for only a split second before she ducked her head to examine his injury.

There were several small cuts across the middle of his foot and one larger slice near his toes. She probed the cuts gently and heard his sharp intake of breath just as she felt a prick to her finger. A small piece of glass protruded from the end of one cut.

She met Kylen's gaze. "This might hurt."

"Remember, 'Vengeance is mine' is God's line not yours. So be gentle." One lid dropped in a bold wink, and her heart gave a little flip.

She grinned and clacked the tips of the tweezers together with an evil pump of her brows.

He chuckled, and she was tempted to join him, but the sight of Daddy moving slowly through the kitchen turned her thoughts to more serious matters. He had finished sweeping and was now filling a mop bucket at her sink.

She forced her eyes to the bottom of Kylen's foot and bent to the task of getting the shards of glass out. "I think you might need to go to the emergency room." She pressed on the cut she had just pulled the glass from. "Did I get it all?"

"Feels like it. I'll be fine."

Outside, a car crunched across the gravel drive, and Taysia glanced up, wondering who it could be.

"That will be the police," Kylen said.

Daddy began to mutter and swish the mop with more vigor. Taysia glanced at him as she stood to get the door. He was blushing! She stopped and arched her brows. "Daddy?"

A loud knock sounded at the front door. "Police! Open up!"

Daddy just kept mopping, face pointed at the floor.

Taysia moved to the door and opened it. Two policemen stood on the porch, guns drawn. “Hi. Please come in. Everything is fine. It was just my dad.”

“Ma’am, I’m Officer Wilkes. This is my partner, Officer Rogers. You’re sure everything is fine?”

“Please come in.” She stepped back out of the way and motioned them inside, not at all sure everything was fine.

Officer Wilkes immediately noticed the bloody footprints. “What happened here?”

Kylen spoke up from where he sat. “Hi, Carl.” He dipped his head. “Tim. I cut myself on some broken glass when I came over to check on Taysia. Dispatch called me, since Taysia told them I lived right next door.”

Apparently convinced the situation was under control, both officers sheathed their weapons.

Rogers pulled out a pen and notepad.

Carl Wilkes took in Daddy silently mopping the kitchen. “Is this the man who broke into your house?”

“Yes—uh, no.” Taysia wanted to pull her hair in frustration. “Well, yes, he was the intruder, but...oh, Daddy, will you just tell me what you are doing here, please? Did you use your key to get in?”

“So you did lock your doors when I told you to earlier?” Kylen interrupted.

Taysia spun toward him in aggravation. “Yes, I

locked the doors." She sighed and rolled her eyes with a "What? Do you think I have a death wish?" glare.

Kylen raised his hands and shrugged.

Everyone in the room looked at Daddy, who turned redder than the apples in the bowl on the counter.

Taysia stomped back to her chair and snatched a Band-Aid from the box.

"Sir, we need to know what you were doing in your daughter's house in the middle of the night." Officer Rogers tapped his pen against the notepad.

Taysia held her breath. Daddy leaned the mop handle against the wall and rubbed his palms down the front of his shirt. "Well..." He licked his lips. "I was at the beach with a...friend."

Taysia sat up straight. Daddy at the beach at this hour of the night? The Band-Aid dangled from her finger, momentarily forgotten.

"And it got kinda late...and I needed to...so I came here instead of going home."

Taysia narrowed her eyes. Was he even speaking English?

"Your car is still idling out front, sir," Officer Rogers said.

"Yeah. I wasn't planning on being here this long."

"Daddy, what are you saying? You just wanted to stop in and check on me? At three thirty in the morning? You're not making any sense!"

Daddy scuffed a toe across the floor. "I didn't say that."

Taysia threw an exasperated glance at Kylen. His face suddenly held a light of understanding. She looked to the other two officers. Both men were doing their level best to suppress grins of mirth. What was she missing? She was now the only one who had no idea why her father was here, right now, at 3:47 a.m., in her living room. Irritation with her father and, in fact, the entire male half of the species made her want to scream.

Officer Wilkes cleared his throat. "I see. Well"—he turned to Taysia—"will you be pressing charges?"

Unbelievable! She opened her mouth to demand that Daddy tell her what was going on.

"Layne." Kylen's tone held a note of warning.

She turned to look at him.

He gave a small shake of his head and mouthed, "Tell you later."

She snapped her mouth shut. Pressing one hand to her forehead, she closed her eyes. "No, Officer. I won't be pressing charges."

"Well, then, if there is nothing more you need, we'll be leaving."

Taysia looked at Daddy, worry niggling like a barbed hook. "No, I don't think we need anything, thank you." Except the return of some sanity.

"See you on Monday, guys." Kylen raised a hand of farewell as the officers left the way they had come.

"Daddy, come sit down, please. I can finish mopping in a minute." Taysia pressed the Band-Aid over Kylen's cut and gestured for his other foot.

"I really best be getting home." Daddy shoved his hands into his pockets.

Kylen hissed as her probing found another splinter of glass. "Easy, Layne. I kinda need that foot for a while longer."

"Sorry." She concentrated on a gentler application of the tweezers.

"Don't swear much, do you, young man? A lesser man'd be scorching the room right about now."

Taysia and Kylen both lifted their heads and looked at each other. Hope pounded in Taysia's chest. She had been praying for this kind of opportunity for months.

Kylen rubbed his temple with one forefinger. "Well, sir, I used to swear with the best of them, but not anymore. Not since I gave my life to the Lord."

Daddy huffed. "Oh, you're one of *them*."

Taysia's heart sank.

Kylen didn't look offended. "If by 'one of them' you mean someone who has found joy and happiness by finally deciding to do things God's way instead of my own, then yes. Giving my life to the Lord was the best decision I ever made."

Taysia could see the sincerity on his face.

Daddy jingled some change in his pocket. "Well, I'll have to admit to admiring a man who stands by his convictions without flinching."

Taysia felt hope, like the first green glimpse of a spring tulip, shooting through the soil of doubt in her heart.

"Well, if you don't want to see me flinch, you better turn your back, because your daughter doesn't have a very good bedside manner." Kylen grinned.

Taysia smacked the side of Kylen's foot in disagreement but ignored his ribbing and spoke to her father. "Daddy, I'm going to church tomorrow. Would you like me to pick you up? You could come with me."

"Nope."

Taysia's hopes died with the ice in his voice.

Daddy's voice softened. "Well, sorry to have caused all this ruckus." His gesture encompassed the floor and Kylen's feet. "But it is late, so I'm gonna head for home now. Good night."

Swallowing her disappointment, Taysia lifted her hand. "Night."

The front door clicked shut, and Daddy's car crunched out of the drive, leaving total silence behind. Taysia could feel Kylen's eyes boring into the top of her head as she applied the last Band-Aid.

"Don't let it get you down, Layne. He'll come around."

She sighed. "I hope so. I think your foot is

done. Can you feel any spot that I need to look at again?"

Kylen palpated first one foot and then the other. "They feel fine. I think you got it all."

"So what was I missing? Everyone seemed to know why Daddy was here but me."

Kylen's chuckle only irritated her more.

"Just think about it. Where was he when I got here?"

Taysia thought for a moment before her eyes widened in sudden understanding. "He needed to use the..."

Kylen nodded. "Yep."

"Oh, for Pete's sake! And I might have never known he was here if I hadn't rearranged the furniture and put that crystal vase on the pedestal." She glanced to where the vase had been displayed, and moaned. "It looked so nice!"

Kylen grinned and eased to his feet. "I better get home. I'll see you at church in the morning."

She saw him to the door. "Thanks for coming to my rescue." She meant the comment to sound flippant.

His face turned serious. "Anytime, Layne. You just call and I'll come running."

She watched him soft-foot across the lawn toward home and knew he meant exactly what he'd said.

Drat the man and his troublesome timing!

Chapter 4

The church gymnasium was loud despite the carpeted walls and cloth ceiling. Bouncing basketballs, squeaking tennis shoes, a stereo pulsing upbeat Christian music, and the buzz of high-energy conversations created a typical youth-group atmosphere.

"Thank you, Mr. Reed!" Taysia shouted over the cacophony to the white-haired man. "We appreciate your support for the youth of our church!" She handed the stoop-shouldered gentleman the box of baked goods he had just paid for and wished again that Daddy would come with her to church. There were some wonderful men he would enjoy getting to know.

Mr. Reed pointed to one hearing-aid-filled ear and shook his head. But the smile on his face said "thank you" as he scuttled out of the gym on rickety legs.

Marie, who was arranging cookies on a tray, looked over and grinned. "Thanks for bringing me, Taysia. This is fun."

Taysia smiled and gave her a one-armed squeeze, glad Marie was enjoying herself.

Blaine stepped up next to them, hands in his pockets, as Tom Quigley snagged a cookie from the tray set out for the youth. The six-foot-six lanky senior stuffed the whole cookie in his mouth and spoke around it. "We're trying to get a pickup game going, Miss Green. We need one more player. Will you play with us?"

Taysia gave Blaine a sly look. "Why don't you ask Blaine here?"

Marie huffed. "Blaine can't pla—oh!" Taysia's elbow connected solidly with one rib.

Tom shrugged and glanced at the floor, face red.

Blaine was quick to come to the young man's rescue. "I'll take my turn at the table now, Taysia. Why don't you go play ball? You can work at trying to get me into shape another time." At Taysia's dark look, he continued, "Tell you what, I'll toss the ball at the beginning of the game."

Taysia rolled her eyes but grinned at him and then turned to Marie. "Do you mind if I play a little ball before we go to lunch?"

Marie waved a hand, her eyes darting toward the court. "No. Go ahead."

Taysia followed her gaze. Reece Cahill stood chatting quietly with one of the other female players, but even as Taysia watched, his focus drifted over the girl's shoulder toward Marie. By the time Taysia turned back to Marie, her receptionist had returned her attention to arranging the cookies on the tray like her life depended on it.

Hmmm...so maybe the breakup hadn't been as easy for Reece as she'd thought. She'd love to see Marie settled in a relationship with a guy like him. She'd have to put the matter to some prayer.

Looking back to Tom, Taysia said, "Alright. I have some gym clothes in my car. Give me five minutes to change, and I'll be there."

Taysia ended up on the "shirts" team, for which she was thankful because the two girls on the "skins" team wore sweatbands around their heads to distinguish them—and she hated wearing a sweatband.

Scooping her hair back into a careless ponytail, Taysia walked onto the court as she cheered her team on. "Alright, guys! Come on, let's do this." She clapped her hands and stepped into the center circle, ready to jump for the ball. Tom Quigley looked down his nose at her from the other side of the line, and she grinned up at him. "How's the weather up there?" She knew he was proud of his height—even hoped to play college ball for Gonzaga next year.

Reaching out, he ruffled her hair playfully and replied, "Don't worry, I won't even jump." Then in an aside to his team he chuckled, "I won't need to."

Taysia's eyes narrowed in a friendly challenge.

"Alright, team, let's whip 'em!" And, as Blaine prepared to toss the ball, she batted her eyelashes coyly in his direction.

"Hey! No fair," yelled one of the players from the other team as the ball rose into the air, arching decidedly in Taysia's favor.

Blaine's crooked toss was to no avail. Tom reached out one long arm and snatched the ball out of the air, and the first points went to the other team.

Still, fifteen minutes later the "shirts" were ahead when Tom's mother called to him that it was time for them to go home. Groans sounded from several of the other players who weren't ready to quit the game yet.

"Bye, Tom." Taysia waved and stepped to the top of the key, dribbling the ball and waiting to see how the players would be redistributed.

Someone spoke from the sidelines. "I'll take his place."

The ball ricocheted off Taysia's foot, jounced across the gym, and clanged into the metal bleachers, causing the teenagers to eye her curiously. Her pulse raced like a rabbit with a coyote on its tail. Why did she let him affect her so?

Kylen Sumner, dressed handsomely in khaki cargo shorts and a black T-shirt that enhanced his dark eyes, stepped onto the court and brought his nose to within an inch of hers, a grin sparkling in his gaze. "You are going down."

She arched her brow and chuckled. "We'll see if you can live up to that big mouth of yours."

He stepped back and smiled at the other players, who, without exception, watched them curiously. "Let's play ball, then." He stripped off his shirt and tossed it aside, stepping between Taysia and her teammates.

Taysia swallowed and refused to allow her gaze to fall.

Her attention settled on Blaine, who had a grim look on his face as he roughly shoved a plate of cookies into a startled patron's hands and plunked the money into the cash box. Marie caught her eye and made her "he's so gorgeous" face, covering her mouth with one hand. Taysia suppressed a smile and looked away, holding out her hands to receive the throw-in from Reece.

The other two girls in the game unashamedly gawked at Kylen as, muscles rippling, he crouched and slid smoothly across the floor, anticipating Taysia's every move.

Taysia feinted one way, then spun, intending to dribble around him the other way, but she collided with the solid wall of his chest, lost complete control of the basketball, and dissolved into a fit of giggles. Kylen grinned and took time to steady her, or he would have had the ball. Luckily Reece recovered it and made the shot.

The game was full of joking and fun. Smack talk reverberated off the gym walls, mixing in with the laughter of players and spectators alike.

Taysia snatched a pass out of the air and made a dash for her basket at the other end of the court. But Kylen loomed before her, reaching for the ball. She headed for the sideline, trying to make it past him as he backed down the court, taunting her. Suddenly he tripped and fell, and Taysia sprawled across his chest in an undignified heap. The ball bounced jauntily toward the middle of the court, the other players laughing and scrambling for it.

They both gulped air as she pushed herself up on one elbow, her face only inches from his. She forced herself to ignore the heat emanating from the place where his arm rested across her back. He had clutched her to him as they fell. To protect her and take the brunt of the impact? She brushed the thought aside. "You're a sweaty cheater!" She jabbed his chest and tried not to smile. Kylen attempted a grin as he flexed first one foot and then the other, but it was more of a wince, and Taysia's eyes widened with sudden chagrin. "Your feet!"

He closed his eyes and heaved a breath through his nose. A garbled sound of acknowledgment was his only reply.

"Come on." She jumped up and reached down to help him stand. "Let's get you home."

He took her hand, but didn't release it once he was on his feet. "Not home. Let's go to the beach for a picnic."

She chewed one side of her lower lip. "I can't, I

have Marie with me." She looked up at him, but when he attempted to lace his fingers through hers, her gaze darted across the gym to Blaine. His eyes were on them, a frown firmly in place. Taysia pulled her hand from Kylen's with some reluctance.

His jaw hardened. "Have a date with Pittman again today?"

"Hey, are you two still playing or what?" one of the teenagers called.

Taysia gave Kylen her best "none of your business" glare, then turned to the group. "We have to go, guys! Thanks for a great game. We should do it again next month after the car wash."

Agreement went around the court, and Taysia headed toward Marie at the baked goods table. Kylen ambled along at her side, slipping his shirt over his head. "Brice, you ready?" he called to a young man talking with a group of girls across the gym.

He lifted his hand in Kylen's direction, said something to the girls that caused a giggle, and then loped across the gym toward them. He had Kylen's dark good looks, but his eyes were a striking green.

"Hi, Brice." Taysia smiled, recognizing Kylen's cousin. "It's nice to see you again." She reached out her hand. "Last time I saw you, Kylen and the rest of the guys from our senior class were stuffing you in your locker."

He grinned and shook her hand. "Yeah, ninth

grade was pretty miserable for me."

Marie glanced up as they approached. "I'm—I—we—" She stuttered to a stop before she even got started, her eyes fixed directly on Brice.

Taysia grinned at Kylen, then turned to Marie. "Marie, this is Brice. He is Officer Sumner's cousin. Brice, Marie is my receptionist at the gym."

Marie stretched out her hand. "Hi." She smiled.

Brice's eyes sparked with pleasure as he raked Marie from head to toe. He took her hand. "Nice to meet you." He lingered over the contact, not letting her hand go. Marie blushed and tried to pull away, but it wasn't until Kylen cleared his throat pointedly that Brice finally dropped her hand.

The basketball landed in the middle of their group, hitting Brice in the knees and rolling off behind him. Brice turned to retrieve it, and Reece was suddenly right there beside Marie, breathing hard and looking more than a little uncomfortable as he waited for Brice to grab the ball. He glanced sideways at Marie. "Hi."

"Hi," she returned. Her voice sounded soft and vulnerable. And Taysia didn't miss the way Marie's feet shifted uneasily.

Brice had the ball now and turned to see who to throw it to.

Reece held up a hand. "Right here. Sorry about that."

"No worries." Brice tossed him the ball, and Reece headed back to the game without another word.

Kylen didn't seem to notice the electrified undertones. He looked at Marie. "I was just trying to talk Taysia into a beach picnic. Brice and I had planned to go there for lunch anyway. What do you say? Sound like fun?"

"Uh, that sounds great." Her eyes widened, and she turned to Taysia sheepishly. "I mean. It's good with me." But Taysia didn't miss the way Marie's gaze darted toward the court, where Reece and the others had resumed the pickup game.

Taysia glanced at Kylen. He wore a look of contrived innocence and arched his brow.

A picnic at the beach did sound like fun. And Marie could probably use the distraction. The day was beautiful. She glanced over at Blaine as she answered, "Just give me a minute. I'll meet you by the door."

Kylen and Brice grinned and high-fived each other like two little boys who'd just been promised a double scoop of their favorite ice cream. Taysia rolled her eyes at them as Marie gathered her bag from under the bake sale table and all three headed across the gym.

Taysia waited for Blaine to finish talking with the lady buying treats from him before she approached, trying to decide what to say. Did she need to say anything? It wasn't like she owed

Blaine an explanation for everything she did. She could go to lunch with whoever she wanted to. But really, she ought to tell him something. He was a nice guy. He deserved at least some sort of explanation.

Mrs. Masters thanked Blaine and picked up her cake, calling for her children as she walked away.

Taysia stepped forward, opened her mouth, paused, and snapped it shut again. Her mind was a blank slate. "I'm going to go now. I'll see you later."

Jaw clenched, he tucked the money into the cash box. Then he looked directly at her. "Taysia, there's something going on between you two, isn't there?"

She swallowed, glancing over her shoulder. Kylen leaned casually against the wall, his eyes deep and black, boring into her as though he could see her very soul. Marie and Brice talked quietly by his side. Taysia sighed. "Blaine, things are complicated between me and Kylen. They've always been complicated."

Blaine picked up a cookie and glared toward Kylen. "He's not good enough for you, Taysia. He never has been."

Taysia reached under the table and pulled out her gym bag, slinging it over her shoulder. "Kylen is the reason I'm saved, Blaine. If it weren't for him..." Her voice trailed off, and she shrugged. "I'll see you later, okay?"

He stuffed the cookie in his mouth and nodded. But his eyes remained on Kylen.

She started away.

"Taysia."

"Yes?" She paused.

"I just don't want to see him hurt you again, you know?" There was pain in his eyes.

She swallowed and nodded.

"Come to dinner at my house tonight? A rain check from last night."

How could she say no when he cared so much for her? "Okay. What time?"

"Six?"

She smiled softly. "I'll be there. Can I bring anything?"

His shoulders relaxed as he slid his hands into his pockets. "Just yourself."

"'Kay. See you then." Another patron approached, taking Blaine's attention, and Taysia stood quietly for a moment, just looking at the floor. Then she glanced up and met Kylen's eyes. He stood erect from the wall, waiting. With one last glance at Blaine, she moved toward Kylen.

Why did she feel like she was heading into a minefield? One misstep on her part and her carefully ordered life could blow apart at any moment.

Taysia scanned the parking lot for Kylen's

squad car as she followed him outside. But Kylen stopped next to a metallic red 1969 Mustang convertible. The top was down. Brice and Marie were already in the backseat.

Her breath caught. Only her favorite vehicle of all time. Taysia took in the lines of the beautiful car, mouth gaping like a Venus flytrap.

Kylen grinned and chucked her chin.

She snapped her mouth shut.

"She's a beaut, huh? I restored her myself."

Taysia ran a hand carefully over the top of the passenger door. "It's gorgeous!"

Brice cringed. "Oh boy, here we go."

"Ahhh! Shhhh!" Kylen clapped one hand over Taysia's mouth, and she turned startled eyes in his direction. "*IT'S*?? You called my baby girl an *it*!" He let go of her mouth, gently patted the side of the car, and cooed, "Don't listen to her, baby, she doesn't know anything."

Taysia couldn't help the smirk as she folded her arms. "Does *she* have a name?"

Kylen dropped the act with a smile as he took her bag and opened the passenger door for her. "Nah. I sure had fun fixing this baby up, though. Great therapy." He moved around to the back and dropped her bag into the trunk, then climbed behind the wheel.

"Therapy? You needed therapy?"

"Mmmm-hmm." He backed smoothly from their space and eased to a stop at the church entrance, glancing both ways before he pulled out onto the road. "Trying to forget this gorgeous blonde I knew back in high school." He said it with an air of nonchalance but cast her a sly glance and a wink.

"Sophia?" she asked innocently.

He snorted. "Not a chance." His face suddenly turned very serious, and he reached over to clasp her hand. "Not a chance."

Taysia's heart lurched as the warmth of his hand settled around hers. She knew she should pull away. What reason did she have to trust him?

Marie leaned forward from the backseat and peered down at their hands. "Ooohh. Nice." She cocked her head and looked up at Kylen. "Now that you are dating my boss, is there any chance you could do something about that ticket you gave me last week?"

Taysia gasped and scrambled to push Kylen's hand away. "Marie, we are not dating!"

Kylen barked a laugh and shook his head at Marie. "No."

Taysia folded her arms, tucking her hands out of sight. The nerve of the girl. Maybe a dock in pay was in order!

Marie sighed and sat back. "I had to give it a try," she yelled over top of the wind.

Still amused over Marie's temerity, Kylen turned into his driveway a few minutes later.

Taysia sat stiffly by his side. He glanced at her as he turned off the key, wondering what troubled her. He caught Brice's eye in the rearview mirror. "Brice, grab the little grill off Mom and Dad's deck out back, would you? I'm just going to grab the cooler." He looked back and forth between the girls.

Taysia, arms still folded, refused to meet his glance.

Marie, on the other hand, batted her eyelashes and stuck out her lower lip in a pleading pose, still begging for him to do something about her ticket.

He almost burst out laughing but shook his head at her instead. "I have stuff for kabobs. Does that sound good? Or should I grab hamburger too?"

Taysia glanced up. "Kabobs are fine. Sounds good."

Marie sighed, apparently having gotten the message that he wasn't going to give in to her cajoling. It was a lesson that could save her life one day. He hoped she would learn from it.

"Kabobs are fine."

"Great, I'll be right back."

It was only a moment before they were on their way again, heading the couple blocks to the beach. Taking in the familiar route, he tapped the steering wheel. He and Taysia had walked this path often that first summer. Until his pride and selfishness ruined their friendship.

He sighed and pulled into a parking spot.

Brice and Marie scrambled out of the back, and Kylen popped the trunk. Taysia sat quietly, taking in the pulsing surf as she tucked a stray hair behind her ear. She had fallen into a melancholy mood. He shouldn't have tried to hold her hand.

Brice and Marie grabbed the lunch supplies from the trunk and headed toward the beach.

Kylen tucked his hands under his legs lest he make things worse. He looked out over the ocean. "I'm sorry. I didn't mean to make you uncomfortable."

She glanced at him. "You didn't do anything to make me uncomfortable. It's just me. I'm so..." She shrugged. "Up in the air right now. With my worries about Daddy and...when Marie said that, I just..."

He swallowed and dug his fingers into the leather of his seat, wishing he could reach for her hand without complicating matters. "Does that mean you are at least thinking about what I said at the gym the other day?" His heart thundered in his ears as he waited.

There was a short pause, and then she chuckled. "No. Not at all."

He looked at her sharply.

She rolled her eyes and then scuttled out of the car, calling, "What do you think has made me so confused lately?"

A slow smile spread across his face as he

followed her out of the car. *Thank You, God!*

The kabobs were some of the best he'd ever tasted. Maybe because his heart was so light. He savored the last piece of meat on his stick as he watched Marie and Brice across the grill. They sat on a large driftwood log and only had eyes for each other. He glanced at Taysia. She was watching the young couple too, a worried look in her eye. As there should be. He sighed. Brice reminded him a lot of himself a few years earlier. He would have to have a talk with him.

Just then Brice looked up. "Want to play some volleyball? There's always a net set up just down there." He pointed down the beach. "And I brought a ball. It's in Kylen's trunk."

Taysia's face brightened, and she looked up at him.

Tossing his kabob stick into the garbage, he stood. "Sure. Sounds like fun."

Brice and Marie formed one team; Kylen and Taysia the other.

Marie set the ball up nicely for Brice, and he sailed into the air and spiked it into the sand just behind Taysia. Marie and Brice high-fived.

Brice pumped his fist. "Oh yeah, baby. We're gonna beat the ol' fogeys."

"That's right!" Marie agreed.

Kylen shook his head in amusement, and beside him Taysia laughed.

A moment later the ball landed out of bounds, and the serve turned over to him and Taysia.

Marie grinned, widened her stance, and bent her knees, ready for the serve. "Don't worry, Brice. They probably serve like pansies."

"Oh, it's on now!" Taysia rested the ball against one hip and pointed a finger at Marie. "You better watch it, girl. I know your boss."

Marie laughed sassily and waved a hand. "She's a pushover. In fact, I'm due for a raise any day now, so you should say something about that to her."

While Marie talked, Taysia served the ball right past her head. The ball landed with a satisfying thud in the sand.

Kylen laughed at the look of astonishment on Marie's face.

"Hey!" Her hands settled on her hips. "That's cheating!"

Taysia grinned. "You should have been playing instead of flapping your jaw, girl."

Marie made a face and tossed the ball back.

Taysia served again and Brice returned it. The ball sailed up high and Kylen ran for it. "Got it!" Taysia called. He tried to stop and back off, but she was watching the ball and crashed into him. Their legs got tangled.

Taysia squeaked, and he grabbed her to him in an attempt to maintain their balance. He failed. They both went down into the sand.

The ball landed in bounds, and Marie and Brice set to celebrating. But suddenly everything around Kylen seemed very far away. Everything except for Taysia. She lay on her back, only inches from his face, her hair fanned out across the sand, her eyes sparkling with amusement. She chuckled and punched him in the arm. "I called it, you goofball!"

Kylen leaned onto one elbow, in no hurry to get up. He stared at a shimmering strand of her hair, remembering a similar day years ago. They had walked to the beach, teasing and jostling. He had chased her. She had fallen, and he had teased that he was going to put sand in her hair. Kylen blinked and refocused on the present.

He took in her face. Smooth eyebrows. Large gray eyes, outlined with dark lashes, turning suddenly serious at his scrutiny. Flushed cheeks. Full, parted lips. He leaned forward. Her breathing stilled and she tensed, clearing her throat softly. *Don't go there, Sumner.* He transitioned his forward momentum into reaching for a handful of sand, forcing his mind on to other avenues. Letting the grains trickle through his fingers, he gave her a wicked grin. Her eyes widened. He could see that same memory flooding her face.

Taysia swallowed thickly. That day on the beach so long ago had been wonderful, full of fun. It had been just before school started. Just before Kylen realized she wasn't popular and that friendship with her would mean hard times for him at Marinville High. Just before she realized how painful love could be.

All Taysia could think was to get away from him. Once again, she was having fun with him. And too much desire coursed through her veins right now. "I really ought to go clean up the lunch things." She struggled to sit up, but one of his legs was pinning her to the ground.

The moment stretched as his face turned serious again, and he watched the grains of sand in his hand cascade back to the beach. Why did he have to be so easy on the eyes? He returned his gaze to her face, and she licked her lips. "Please, Ky. Let's just clean up the lunch stuff." She didn't think she would have the strength to resist if he was tempted to kiss her again.

Kylen hopped up and reached a hand down. "I'll come help you." As he dusted sand from himself, he called over to Brice and Marie, "We're going to go clean up the lunch things. We'll be ready to go in a bit."

Taysia hurried toward the picnic site, adrenaline making her legs tremble. She wouldn't kid herself. There was no way she was attractive enough to keep the handsome Kylen Sumner's attention for any length of time. Sure, he was home and claiming interest in her, but beautiful girls like Sophia Clinesmith were really more his type. And it was best she remember that. She'd forgotten it one too many times already.

Quickly she scooped all the leftovers into the cooler and headed for the car. Kylen followed carrying the small grill and popped the trunk for her. She stuffed the cooler inside. As she pulled back, her hand got caught in one strap of her bag and her Bible fell out, spilling bulletins and notes everywhere.

"Oh, bother!" She began to gather the papers together, placing today's bulletin on the top. Her hands stilled as notes from Pastor's sermon arrested her attention. Pastor had quoted Samuel Taylor Coleridge. "And the devil did grin, for his darling sin is pride that apes humility." This morning's sermon had been all about pride, and she had brushed it aside because she knew she didn't have a problem with thinking more highly of herself than she ought; in fact, she was quite the opposite. But was her "humility" actually pride in disguise? Was it actually pride refusing to allow Kylen back into her heart? Fear of humiliation if he decided, once again, that he'd be better off with someone else? Wanting to protect herself?

Kylen stood behind her waiting so he could put the grill into the trunk. "Layne, you okay?" he asked.

She quickly shuffled the papers together. "I'm fine." She brushed past him as verses from Philippians 3 marched through her head. *But one thing I do: Forgetting what is behind and straining toward what is ahead, I press on toward the goal to win the prize for which God has called me heavenward in Christ Jesus.*

She clenched her fists and sank down onto a driftwood log. She didn't want to forget what he had done to her. She didn't ever want herself to be vulnerable to him again. She had forgiven him and was pressing on; wasn't that enough? She was serving God, doing her best to love and help others. *Isn't that enough, God? I just don't want to be hurt again.*

Kylen eased down on the log beside her. She leaned forward, resting her elbows on her knees and cupping her chin in one hand. The waves pulsed a soothing rhythm, and she let her eyes fall closed. *Lord, I don't know if I'm being prideful or not. I do have a hard time believing Kylen could really be attracted to me. And I know I don't want to get hurt again. And I'm so attracted to him that it makes it really hard. What if we start dating and he dumps me again?* She sighed. *Just help me to find Your way through all of this. And if there is sin in my heart, show me, Lord. And help me to be willing to let go of it.*

Kylen reached over with one hand and began to massage the muscles along her back and at the base of her neck. He cleared his throat. "Layne, I need to ask you something." He paused, and she reached for a shell in the sand between her feet. "Do you think there is any chance at all that you will ever care for me again? Trust me?"

She tensed and looked out across the ocean to the horizon, her pulse skittering like a colt in the cool morning. *Yes, that's what I'm afraid of.* She swallowed and looked back down at the sand. "Kylen, I just don't know if I can go there again."

He stiffened, and his hand paused at the base of her neck. Then he placed his hands on his knees and stood. "I see. I'll go get Marie and Brice."

Pain clenched Taysia's chest until she could hardly breathe as she watched Kylen walk slowly down the beach, his hands shoved deep into the pockets of his shorts. She dashed at the tears on her cheeks with the flats of her fingers and headed back to the car to wait for them.

Kylen was strong. And there would be plenty of women for him to choose from. He would be fine. And she had Blaine. They would both be fine.

Chapter 5

Kylen walked down the beach a way and then paused, looking out over the endless motion of the water. He sighed and rolled his head from side to side as he let his mind wander back over the years to high school.

That first summer, he and Taysia had become friends almost immediately. Their friendship had quickly blossomed into romance, and he had finally worked up his nerve and kissed her under the grape arbor in her backyard. That night she had shared her fears with him. She had never been popular at school. She'd always just been "Chubby Taysia Green." Earlier that year, before he arrived, she had determined to lose weight and help women do the same in the future, but she knew nothing would change at school. She told him she was afraid when school started he would turn his back on her, because no one was going to like him if he hung out with Fatty Four-Eyes. He had assured her nothing could be further from the truth.

Kylen huffed a breath of disgust with himself and scuffed his toe through the sand. That first year, things had been okay between him and Taysia for a while, but eventually the ribbing he took at school for hanging around her got to him, and he'd slowly stopped sitting with her, walking home with her, talking with her.

The hurt in her big gray eyes the first time he'd passed her by in the cafeteria to sit instead with the football players and cheerleaders pierced his heart. The first time she called a greeting to him across their lawns, and he merely waved and headed to the beach with his new friends, her shoulders had slumped. He'd felt like a cad, but he'd valued popularity more than his relationship with her.

Soon, like a dog that gets cuffed every time its owner is around, she carefully began evading him. Even during the summers, she made a point of staying as far from him as possible. And, selfishly, he hadn't given her a serious thought until the night of their senior prom.

Taysia had been so beautiful that night.

Her date was Darwin Schwartz, a punk rocker with a tattoo of a dragon on his neck and a silver earring that dangled down so far it bumped against his shoulder. Darwin hadn't been at the prom for fifteen minutes before he was well on his way to being drunk.

None of the jocks had been able to tear their

eyes off Taysia, all of them wishing they'd had enough guts to be the first to break the "Taysia Green Taboo" and ask her to the prom themselves. Kylen included. Her sapphire-blue dress hung just off slender, tanned shoulders, and a small sapphire-and-diamond pendant graced the hollow of her throat. Somewhere in her high school years, Taysia had learned she couldn't be anybody but herself, and she'd stopped trying to impress the popular people. She mingled around the room chitchatting with her friends, and everyone in the room noticed her exquisite beauty. It was a beauty that emanated not only from her outward appearance but from an inner confidence. The fact that Taysia was unaware of it only added to her allure.

On that night Kylen knew she was the most beautiful girl he'd ever laid eyes on. His date, Sophia Clinesmith, had known it too and hadn't liked the way Kylen watched Taysia across the room.

Sophia waited until Taysia stopped by the punch bowl and then approached her. Filling her own cup, she angled Taysia a smile. "Taysia! You're looking fab tonight!" She reached out as though to give her a hug and sloshed punch down the front of Taysia's dress. Apologizing profusely, she swiped at the stain with a wad of napkins from the table. Everyone in the room knew the truth.

Taysia's eyes darted to Kylen, a blush staining

her cheeks as she pushed Sophia's hands away and whispered that everything was fine and not to worry. Backing away from the refreshment table, she glanced frantically around the room.

Kylen followed her gaze and saw Darwin cavorting drunkenly on the dance floor with a girl wearing black makeup and leather. He turned back to see Taysia fleeing the room.

He glared at Sophia. "That was cold, Sophia. Couldn't stand the fact that she is twice as beautiful as you ever will be?" The words were hard, cutting. He meant them to be. Sophia burst into tears, covered her face with trembling hands, and flounced away. Several of her girlfriends rushed to console her with embraces and glares in Kylen's direction. Kylen hesitated only a split second before he pushed through the surprised murmur of his classmates and ran after Taysia.

Darwin must have driven her, because she was striding through the rain, swiping at her cheeks with one hand. He ran for his car and pulled out of the parking lot. Driving half a block ahead, he stopped at the curb and jumped out, turning to face her as she approached.

"Go away, Kylen! You are the last person on earth I want to talk to right now!"

"Taysia, just let me drive you home. It's cold and raining, and it's over two miles to your house." By this time she was abreast of his car. She ignored him and tried to push past him, but he stepped into her path, resting his hands on her upper arms. "Come on, Layne, just let me drive you home."

She folded her arms, stepped back, and dropped her gaze to the sidewalk. "I can't go home, Kylen."

He frowned. "Why not?"

She swiped at a tear with the flats of her fingers, then refolded her arms without ever looking up. "I just can't. My parents..."

Understanding dawned. She didn't want her parents to know. "Fine." He took her by the arm, leading her to the passenger side of his car. "Come to my house, then. My parents are gone on business. At least you can have a warm shower and get into something dry. You can sneak home later."

She sank down into the seat without protest and leaned her head back. The minutes ticked off silently as he drove, the only sound that of the wipers methodically swishing across the windshield. He swallowed nervously, hating the silence. "You looked beautiful tonight." The words were a surprise. He hadn't meant to voice the thought aloud.

She grimaced. "Shut up, Kylen."

He pulled into the drive of his dark house and glanced over at her. "Taysia?"

She turned her head on the headrest and looked at him, her gray, tear-bright eyes shining luminously in the moonlight.

He swallowed convulsively, his heart

beginning to beat hard in his chest. He reached out and stroked her cheek with the backs of his fingers. “I mean it, Layne. You were the most beautiful girl there tonight.”

She closed her eyes and did not pull away from his touch.

It felt right when he leaned across the car and kissed her. Memories of their first tender kiss and that whole wonderful first summer when they had simply been two friends falling in love clouded his thinking. It felt right when they stumbled into the house and he pulled her up the stairs into his bedroom. Momentarily gone was the distance that Kylen had placed between them. It was as if they had never stopped being friends, being in love. Everything had felt right until it was over, and then he had known he’d made the biggest mistake of his life. Taysia didn’t meet his eyes as she got up and slipped back into her stained, wet gown and left. He’d been too angry with himself for taking advantage of her to stop her. Besides, what could he say?

He had walked to his window, watching as she darted across the lawn and eased through her back door.

If things had been strained between them before, they were even more so after that day. He remembered making snide comments about her as she passed him in the halls, loud enough for her to hear. He remembered the hurt acceptance that always haunted her eyes whenever he dared to actually look at her. There hadn't been much of the year left, but he remembered he'd been cold and demeaning.

He had been a sophomore in college, and hadn't seen Taysia for two years, when he had attended church with his roommate and his eyes had been opened to his need of a Savior. His hunger for the Word had been voracious, and he had submersed himself into it, reading and studying it avidly.

By the time summer break rolled around, he had known he needed to make things right with Taysia.

As he drove the road home that year, he had prayed God would give him the words to express his heartfelt regret. That opportunity came when he saw Taysia heading out for her jog one day. He followed.

They jogged quite a ways down the beach to a lonely stretch not often accessed by tourists. She had to know he was jogging behind her by now. "Taysia!" he called.

She thought about simply ignoring him—he knew because she kept jogging for about ten feet before she stopped and spun toward him. She glanced around at the empty beach with a telling glance and arched a slender brow in his direction. "Afraid someone might see you talking to me?" She hauled in a breath of the fragrant, salty air, looking out over the ocean to the flat horizon beyond. "What do you want, Kylen?"

"I want to apologize."

She cast him a swift glance, surprise evident on her face.

He went on, undaunted. "I've become a Christian, Taysia, and I know the things I've done to you must have hurt you terribly. I should never have thrown away our friendship like I did in the first place. You meant more to me than that; *mean* more to me than that. The night of the prom—we should never have—*I* should never have—well, I'm sorry. I stole something from you that night, and I know it doesn't change the past, but for what it's worth, I'm sorry."

Taysia laughed derisively and stepped right up to him. "You know what you can do with your apology, Kylen Sumner?" Quick as lightning she looped one leg behind him and shoved his chest hard. "You can eat it!"

He staggered backward trying to catch his balance, but there was a piece of driftwood just behind him. He went down hard. His head cracked against a rock beneath the surface of the sand, and blackness skittered across his vision.

Squinting, he looked up to see Taysia leaning over him. "Oh, I'm sorry, I didn't mean it! Kylen, are you alright?" Her hands fluttered around his face in agitation. "Kylen?"

He groaned and rolled his head from side to side, determining the extent of the damage.

"Lie still! Kylen, lie still." She adjusted his head to an angle and peered at the cut behind his ear.

"Don't move." He heard her splash into the waves, then felt her kneel beside him again.

He grimaced and sucked in a breath as salt water hit the wound.

"Hold still!" She bent closer, examining his head. "You're going to need stitches."

He moaned. He couldn't help it; no other words would form.

She grabbed his T-shirt and ripped a piece of cloth from it, pressing it against the flow of blood.

He opened one eye and raised an eyebrow, forcing words past the throb. "May I move now, Nurse?"

She rolled her eyes. He grinned, sat up, and reached to take over pressing the material to his head. When she began to pull away, he captured her hand.

"Taysia, please forgive me." All levity gone, he implored her with his eyes. "The way I treated you was so wrong. I've asked God to forgive me, but I would really like it if you would forgive me too."

Her expression changed. Hardened. "I'll think about it."

His shoulders slumped.

"Kylen! You've no idea what I've been through because of you!" She folded her arms defensively. "Yet you waltz back into my life and expect to make everything better with a few words?"

He sighed and dropped his hand and blood-soaked cloth into his lap.

"Keep that pressed to your head, you're still bleeding."

Absentmindedly, he raised his hand. "You're right, Layne. I have no right to demand anything from you. I only hope one day you will be able to forgive me for the pain I've obviously caused you."

She pursed her lips. "Fine. Do you think you'll be able to make it to the hospital? Or do you want me to drive you?"

He waved a hand. "Go. I'll be fine."

Slowly she got to her feet and turned to leave.

"Layne?"

"What?"

"I just want you to know Jesus is the answer. You talked about making everything better with just a few words. Well, giving my life over to Him was the best thing I ever did. Those few words I prayed really did make everything better. I'll pray that one day you will find that out too."

Without a word or gesture of acknowledgment, she had turned and jogged back down the beach, taking his heart with her...

Kylen sighed. After all these years, his actions were still coming back to haunt him. He picked up a piece of driftwood and hurled it back into the ocean. At least Layne had found a relationship with the Lord. That was one good thing that had come from the mess he'd made in the past. He sighed and clasped his hands behind his head. Elbows wide, he stared out across the ocean.

Lord, I know I don't deserve her. Maybe she will never be able to trust me again. But it would be really great if You could change her heart toward me. If she is the woman You have for me, then help her to see that I'm different now because of my relationship with You. And help me to continue putting the past behind me, Lord. I can't change it, so help me to move on and do better with my future.

His heart felt lighter, and as he headed down the beach to get Brice and Marie, he knew he wasn't ready to give up on a relationship with Taysia. He would just have to prove to her that he was a changed man.

Taysia hopped out of the car as soon as it came to a stop. "Thanks for the ride."

Kylen pulled the lever to open the trunk and got out. "You sure I can't take you to the church to get your car?"

"No." She would walk the mile to church later to get her car before her date with Blaine. But she was careful not to mention that. She started to reach for her bag, but Kylen beat her to it and gestured her up the walk to her house. She turned to the couple in the backseat. "Bye, Marie. See you tomorrow. Brice, it was nice to meet you again."

The couple waved, but barely took their eyes

off each other to say goodbye.

Taysia swallowed and turned away from the car reluctantly. She just didn't want to see Marie get hurt.

Kylen placed a hand gently on her back and guided her up the steps. "Don't worry. I'll talk to him."

Relieved, Taysia looked up at him as she fumbled for her keys. "Thanks. I just don't want to see her hurt."

He touched her arm, stilling her before she could enter the house.

Her pulse quickened at the serious look on his face.

"Layne." He cleared the gravel out of his throat. "I know I've done some really low things. And I can understand why you are struggling with trusting me. But I want you to know I'm not ready to give up yet. From the moment I laid eyes on you right there"—he nodded to the weeping willow just down the drive—"I knew you were special." He gently traced her brow as he tucked a stray strand behind her ear.

Heart thundering, her mouth opened and shut like a fish out of water. How to respond?

"You don't have to say anything." He shook his head. "I know I've got a lot of ground to make up. But I'm going to show you Jesus really has changed me. And I'm going to pray that God will help you forget what lies behind us and instead look at what our future together can hold."

He slipped his hands into his pockets, stepped back with a wink, and started for the car.

Taysia dropped her bag in the foyer and collapsed against the door as it clicked shut behind her. Her head tipped back and landed against the wood with a soft thud. A small whimper escaped her throat as she looked across her house to the grape arbor she could see through the sliding door. "Lord? I need a little help here."

Kylen felt like whistling as he bounded down the walk. *Thanks, Lord!* All the way home he'd prayed that he would find the courage to tell her he wasn't ready to give up.

He rounded the end of the convertible and started for the driver's door, but stilled. In the backseat, Brice was plastered against Marie, one arm around her shoulders. His other hand rested on her lap toying with her fingers.

Kylen cleared his throat pointedly. Brice glanced up and, at the look on Kylen's face, reluctantly removed his arm and scooted a bare inch away from Marie. Kylen kept glaring until, inch by inch, Brice scooted properly to his side of the car. Marie clasped her hands and bit her lip, unusually quiet. The silence remained thick all the way to Marie's house, and when Kylen returned to the car after walking her to her door,

Brice was slumped in the front passenger seat, one foot resting on the dash.

Kylen slid behind the wheel and backed out of the drive.

The air whistling past their heads was loud and made conversation nearly impossible, but Kylen knew he couldn't let him out of the car without saying something to him. He pulled to a stop by the side of the road just before Brice's house. Brice looked at him questioningly.

Kylen turned to face him. "Listen, Brice, I know you are not going to like this, but I want you to be careful with Marie."

Brice rolled his eyes and looked away. "I was just holding her hand."

Kylen wasn't going to let him off that easy. "It was more than that and you know it. Look, I'm speaking from experience here. I know what it's like to make a mistake with a girl. And you will only have regrets later. I just want to spare you—and her—that pain."

Brice chewed one fingernail, refusing to answer or meet Kylen's gaze.

Kylen sighed and started the car forward, rolling slowly into Brice's drive.

Brice scrambled out of the car.

"Brice."

He stopped, at least waiting to hear what Kylen would say, if not facing him.

"Earlier at church I heard you ask Jenny Sanchez to dinner on Friday night. And an hour later, you're snuggled so close to Marie a piece of paper couldn't have fit between you. You are not being fair to either one of those girls. And frankly, I'm disappointed in your behavior."

Brice's shoulders sagged slightly at that last statement. Good. Maybe it would get him to thinking about his actions.

Kylen started the motor. "See you next week." *God, get through to him. He is so much like I was. Help him to see sooner than I did that Your way is always the best way*. He pulled out onto the road and added a prayer about his next destination. *Help Sophia to see reason. Help her to agree to a settlement so this issue will be settled for Layne and she won't have this lawsuit hanging over her head*.

Fifteen minutes later he turned into the parking lot of the Pacific Café, where he was to meet her. He was a few minutes early. But when he stepped out onto the dining deck that overlooked the azure ocean, Sophia was already there, leaning against the rail in a pose that made him wonder if she'd mistaken this for a model shoot.

Her curve-hugging black dress could have been a tube sock in a former life. And red stiletto heels increased her height by at least four inches. Seeing him, she flipped her hair provocatively and sashayed his way.

He swallowed his distaste. What had he ever seen in her?

"Kylen, dahling!" Somewhere in her travels, Sophia had picked up a fake southern drawl. She took his hand, gave her body a quick spin so she was wrapped in his arm, and peered up into his face. "You're early. Ah'm glad, because now Ah know you've missed me as much as Ah've missed you this past week."

That was all he needed, for her to think he'd rushed over to see her. Setting her from him firmly, he said, "Actually, I had to drive Brice home, and his house is closer to here than mine, so that's why I'm a little early. Shall we find a table?"

"Whatever you say, dahling." She giggled, grabbing his hand.

Pulling away, he shoved both hands deep into his pockets. He should have done this over the phone like he'd wanted to. She was the one who'd insisted they meet to talk about the lawsuit.

Undeterred, Sophia wrapped one of her arms through his and clutched his bicep. "There's a cozy table right ovah here in the corner, Ky." She dragged him toward an intimate, curtained enclave.

Kylen suppressed a growl. "The sun's so beautiful today. How about this table right here?" He pulled out a chair at a table in the middle of the deck.

She didn't sit. "But Ah thought..."

Kylen sat in the chair opposite the one waiting for Sophia and scanned the ocean horizon.

With a huff, Sophia sank into her seat.

The waiter approached, and Kylen spoke. "Just iced tea for me. And separate tickets, please." He wanted her to get the message loud and clear. This was a business meeting, not a date.

Sophia sighed. "Uh...Ah'll have the same."

Momentary guilt touched his conscience. She had probably waited to eat until now. "You can eat if you are hungry."

She batted away the idea with a flip of her wrist. "Ah need to watch mah waistline, anyhow."

His eyes narrowed. "When did you pick up such a southern drawl? Did you move south for a while?"

"No." Her face heated and she grinned at him. "Is it bugging you? To be honest, I've been trying some method acting for a role in a movie I'm hoping to get." All traces of her accent had dropped off.

He smiled. "There's the Sophia I know."

She leaned forward sultrily. "You could get to know me better."

He obviously needed to make things really clear to her. "Listen, Sophia. I need you to know I came back home to convince Taysia to give me a second chance."

One slim penciled brow disappeared under her bangs. "I didn't know there had been a first chance."

His shoulders sagged. "Yeah, well, that's my fault. And I'm hoping she'll forgive me, because

I'm in love with her." There, he'd said it. *Maybe should have waited until after we negotiated the lawsuit.*

The waiter set their drinks on the table. Like a drought victim, Sophia snatched hers up, took three long gulps, and plunked the glass down with a thud. A plastic smile hardened her face. "Well...well, I hope everything works out for you."

Kylen relaxed. She had taken the news better than he thought she would. Ever since he'd returned to town, she'd been making clear what she wanted. Never mind that Jim Saunders, the father of her son, still lived in town. They apparently weren't together right now.

Kylen rubbed his palms against his knees. "So, about the lawsuit. You know your claims won't hold up in court, Sophia. There is no way Taysia can be blamed for someone leaving garbage in her parking lot."

"Oh, posh!" A flick of her wrist waved him to silence. "You know that's not true."

Kylen kept his face bland, but he knew she had a point. Some of the lawsuits won in court these days were absolutely ridiculous.

"Tell you what." She ran a manicured finger around the rim of her glass. "For a hundred thousand, I'll settle out of court."

Kylen leaned back and clasped his hands behind his head. It was going to be a long afternoon.

Taysia arrived at Blaine's apartment five minutes late.

Blaine opened the door before she finished knocking, relief etched on his face.

"Sorry I'm late." The words felt lame even as they rolled off her tongue.

"Don't worry about it." He let her in, took her coat, and gestured toward the dining room. "Barbecued salmon and baby reds, just like I promised you." He shut the door with a soft click.

Suddenly she knew the feeling a convict had when the jail door shut behind him for the first time. *Get a grip, get a grip...* "Smells wonderful." She forced a smile and tried to look like she meant it. She wasn't hungry; didn't know if she could force one bite past the stranglehold of oh-what-am-I-doing-here that clenched her throat.

He stepped past her. "Come in, come in. Everything's ready. I just need to pull the salmon off the grill. Have a seat and I'll be right in."

Taysia eyed the candlelit table with trepidation. She hated this taking-friendship-to-the-next-level business. Why was she so leery? She loved Blaine, didn't she? Sure, she didn't have the whoa!-my-heart-thinks-this-is-a-flamenco-party reactions that she did to Kylen. But that was just because Kylen was...Kylen. "And I won't think of him any more tonight!"

"Who?"

She gasped and spun around.

Blaine, large red lobster-claw potholders on his hands, gripped a steaming tray of salmon garnished with lemon wedges.

"No one. Oh, Blaine, everything looks delicious." He really had gone all out, and here she was thinking about Kylen. Guilt traipsed through her chest. "Is there something I can do to help?"

He set the salmon on the table and hurried into the kitchen. "No. Really," he called. "Please sit. I'll just get the sparkling cider and we'll be all set."

Taysia sank into her chair and took in the fare. Inhaled. Rolled her shoulders. Exhaled. She could do this. She was moving on with her life, and this was how it was done. Kylen was in the past. This was here and now.

Blaine hurried in, wisps of white vapor still rising from the top of the open cider bottle, and she smiled. "Everything looks wonderful, Blaine."

And it was. She surprised herself by eating everything on her plate and even taking seconds on the salmon. Finally, pushing back from the table, she groaned audibly. "I don't think I can walk, and I have classes to teach in the morning."

He grinned. "I'm glad you liked it. Have time for a movie and some chocolate fudge cake?"

Taysia wanted to go home, but the puppy-dog pleading look in his eyes and the reminder to herself that she was trying to move on made her stay.

Two hours later she stood at the door saying goodbye. "Everything was great, Blaine. Thanks for a fun night."

"Sure." He took her hand and studied her mouth openly.

Yes. Kiss me. I'm trying to move on here.

But he just stood there, gnawing his lip nervously and staring at her mouth.

She was just about to reach up and kiss him herself when he leaned in.

Finally! Moving on. She closed her eyes and tilted her head up, resigned and waiting.

He kissed her softly, hesitantly, then stepped back and squeezed her hand. "Have a good week. I'll come by Friday night?"

"O-o-okay. See you then." Disappointment coursed through her. Shouldn't she have at least felt a little excitement from their first kiss? With a sigh she headed for her car.

Kylen was sitting in her porch swing when she pulled into the drive.

The flamenco started in her chest, setting her nerves to tingling. The car stopped with a jerk, sending gravel skidding under the tires. She yanked on the emergency brake and snatched up her purse.

He stood as she got out of the car and sauntered toward her.

She swallowed, resenting the fact that just the

sight of this man made her feel more than a kiss from Blaine had. “What are you doing here?” she snapped.

He blinked. “Just making sure you made it home safe.”

“Well, I’m here! Safe.” She gave a little twirl to prove it.

He grinned. “I can see that. Date with Pittman didn’t go so well, huh?”

She scalded him with a look as she marched up the steps. How had he even known where she was?

Kylen held his hands up in an I-surrender pose. “I’m going home. But I left something for you by your door. Don’t trip on it.” He stepped over the flower bed and disappeared into the darkness.

Keys in her hand, Taysia looked down. A single white rose wrapped in pink tissue paper lay on the welcome mat, the glow from her porch light casting shadows around it.

Like melting chocolate, her peeve slipped away and puddled at her feet.

She stooped and lifted the rose to inhale the fragrance, staring into the darkness in the direction Kylen had disappeared.

This moving-on business is never going to work. With a groan she pushed open her door.

Chapter 6

For two weeks Kylen did little things like the rose. She would step out onto her deck and find a bouquet of wildflowers or a chocolate bar. One morning he knocked at the door and handed her a steaming cup of java from the little stand down the street—tall vanilla macchiato, skinny, no whip, just like she liked it. How had he known? She'd bet Marie had blabbed, but for once her lips were sealed. Twice, he had small bouquets delivered to her at work. Marie gushed and told everyone who came by the front desk that Miss Green was in love. And for some reason she couldn't grasp, Taysia had been unable to deny it.

This Monday morning, anticipation hurried her steps as she climbed out of her car and headed into Mom's Gym. Nothing had been on her porch, or in her mailbox. No dark-eyed police officer had shown up on her stoop to hand her coffee. *But he hasn't missed a day of gift-giving for two weeks.*

To her disappointment, during that time he'd kept his distance, only saying hello at church with a slow, warm smile, or waving to her from his window as she pulled into her drive. Even when he'd brought her the coffee, all he'd said was, "Have a nice day, Layne."

She jogged up the walk to Mom's Gym, stopped, took a calming breath, and did her best to walk nonchalantly into the reception area.

Marie chomped a large wad of gum. As she caught sight of Taysia, her eyes lit up and she blew a huge bubble, smacking it loudly before she raised her eyebrows.

Taysia's heart double thumped. She scanned the counter. Empty. Her pulse stilled. "Oh. Good morning, Marie."

"Morning, Taysia," she said with a cheeky grin.

Taysia held her breath and waited as she scanned the list of classes and clients for the day. Surely something had come this morning, and if so, Marie would be sure to tell her about it. Some news glimmered in her eyes.

"Mrs. Sanchez called to say she won't be able to make it to Third Trimester Toning today. She thinks she might be in labor."

Taysia's shoulders slumped. "Oh...how nice. We'll need to remember to pray as a class for her. Mark that on the top of my agenda for that class today, would you?"

"Sure." Marie popped her gum, the sassy glint still in her eyes.

Taysia finally gave in to her curiosity with a chuckle. "All right, where is it? Your paycheck is in serious jeopardy, girl."

Marie laughed out loud. "Hustle on down to your office, Miss G. And it's a doozy, let me tell you." She paused, then hurried on. "I read the card. Hope you don't mind. I wasn't going to tell you, but Pastor's been talking about honesty at church, so I thought I better 'fess up."

Taysia, already two steps toward her office, stopped and spun back, her gym bag whispering against her leg.

Like a puppy caught with its paws on the garbage can, Marie hung her head and looked at Taysia through her eyebrows.

Taysia arched a brow, but couldn't think of a thing to say in the face of the soul-eyed confession but "You're forgiven. Just don't do it again, please?"

Marie nodded, shoulders relaxing, her quick grin back in place. "Thanks." Then she waved Taysia forward. "Go. It's gonna knock your socks right off."

At her office, Taysia peered around the door as she pushed it open, eyes widening in pace with the expanding view.

On her desk sat a huge bouquet of purple-hued roses interspersed with lupine, baby's breath, and greenery. But what caught her attention were the large clusters of green and purple grapes that cascaded down the front of the crystal vase.

A card poked from the top of the arrangement, and she plucked it out with trembling fingers.

In bold scrawl Kylen had written, "Young love is a flame; very pretty, often very hot and fierce, but still only light and flickering. The love of the older and disciplined heart is as coals, deep-burning, unquenchable. (Henry Ward Beecher.) I'm not going anywhere. Love, Kylen."

Her breath caught in her throat, and tears pricked the backs of her eyes. "Oh, Ky." One hand floated to her mouth as she sank into her chair. Equal amounts of fear and happiness set her pulse to pounding and her mouth stretching from ear to ear. *Heaven help me, I think I'm falling for him again.* Her whole body trembled, and she leaned back with a chuckle. "I have to go teach class, and I'm a total basket case!" She sat in contemplative, sloppy-grinned silence for several minutes before slapping her knees and standing to get ready. "Get a grip, girl. Just get a grip."

Her phone rang as she was headed out the door. She glanced at her watch. Only two minutes to class time. She really should let it go to voice mail. *But what if it's Kylen?* Jogging the five steps to her desk, she snatched up the phone and pressed the talk button. "Hello?"

"Taysia?"

"Daddy? Oh!" She slapped one palm to her forehead. She was supposed to have had breakfast with him this morning! In her hurry to get to the office and see Kylen's gift, she'd forgotten all about it. "I'm so sorry, Daddy. I totally forgot about breakfast."

"That's alright." He chuckled. "I thought maybe you were just getting me back for dinner the last time."

She smiled, her heart sinking a little at the reminder of his absentmindedness. "No, Daddy. I would never do that."

"Well." He cleared his throat. "Can we do dinner? There's something important I really need to talk to you about."

Fear zinged through her. "Uh, yeah, sure." What could he need to talk to her about? She squeezed the base of her neck. "Dinner sounds fine. What time?"

"How about six thirty? Fisherman's Wharf?"

"Sure. I'll be there. I promise not to forget this time."

"Good. See you then."

"Love you, Daddy."

He cleared his throat. "See you tonight."

She hung up and stood staring at the phone for a long minute, massaging her lower lip as she tried to think what Daddy could need to talk to her about so urgently.

With a sigh of resignation, she turned and headed to her class. She would find out soon enough.

Taysia arrived at Fisherman's Wharf just before six thirty. The parking lot was off to one side of the restaurant, and she pulled into a space overlooking the ocean. Here, tall grass swayed closest to the lot, giving way farther out to the unrelenting sand and the pulsing surf. A gull hopped along the beach, cocking his head this way and that as he looked and listened for an ill-fated, bite-sized beach inhabitant.

Climbing out of the car, Taysia pressed her skirt down as the wind snatched at it, swirling it around her ankles. Her sandals clicked noisily on the stone tiles in the restaurant entry.

"Good evening." A waiter smiled at her. "How many in your party this evening?"

She adjusted her purse strap on her shoulder. "There will be two of us. I'm here to meet my father. Is there a single, older man seated already? I'm not sure if I'm here first or not."

He scanned a list on the podium in front of him. "Are you Taysia Green?"

"Yes."

He smiled. "Right this way."

"Thank you." She followed him through an archway with a swordfish hanging above it and dogged his footsteps past several linen-covered tables to one in the corner where Daddy sat waiting.

He smiled. "Hi, sweetheart." He stood and

pulled out a chair for her.

Taysia pushed down the trepidation thundering in her chest. Whatever he had to tell her, she could take it. "Hi, Daddy." She kissed his cheek before she sat.

The view from their window snagged her interest as Daddy moved around to his side of the table to sit. Several sailboats dotted the horizon, crisp white triangular sails bulging in the breeze. One that was closer in bobbed in the waves. On the beach, a young boy threw a ball out into the surf for his golden retriever to fetch. The dog bounded into the water, ears flapping like a bird trying to take flight.

"Beautiful, huh?"

Daddy's words focused her attention on his face. "Yes." She took a sip of water, her ice tinkling against the glass. "Sorry, again, about breakfast." She set the cup down, playing with the moisture that dampened its exterior.

Daddy rubbed his hands together nervously. "Don't worry about it. Listen, honey, I'm going to get right to the point, because she could be back at any moment."

Taysia lifted her head. "Who?" Even as she asked the question, she noticed there were three glasses of water on the table, and the one next to Daddy had lipstick on the rim.

"Loraine." Daddy held up his hands to stop her barrage of questions. "Just listen for a minute."

Forcing her mouth to shut and her hands to settle in her lap was the hardest thing Taysia had done in a long time.

"I met her at the senior center. Her name is Loraine and—oh! Here she is." He stood and pulled out the chair next to him.

Taysia looked in disbelief at the distinguished woman who settled into the waiting seat. The lady glanced up, a smile twinkling in her blue eyes. "Hello, dear." She stretched an age-spotted hand out to Taysia. "I'm Loraine. I'm sure Dale has told you all about me by now. It's so nice to meet you. You have such a *wonderful* father!"

Taysia took her hand automatically, but her eyes fixed on Daddy as he resumed his seat. "Well—I—but—" Taysia sputtered.

Daddy took Loraine's hand and arched a don't-you-dare-make-a-scene eyebrow. "Loraine is the reason I forgot about our dinner plans the other night. And I was with her on the beach the night of my"—he cleared his throat—"late-night visit to your house."

Loraine tittered and leaned across the table. "Early morning is more like it. Dale told me all about that—I can't believe you called the police! Of course, what else were you to do, you poor dear. Thinking someone had broken into your house!" She laid her hand over Taysia's. "I've made him promise that in the future when the mood strikes us to stay up to all hours, he will stop at a convenience store or something, instead of scaring you spitless!"

Taysia's mouth gaped. She couldn't help herself. *Daddy has a girlfriend! He's not getting Alzheimer's or something! Oh, thank You, God! She's beautiful! A little younger than Mom would be now, but still close to Daddy's age.*

Loraine's hand came up to cover her mouth. "You poor thing, he hasn't told you, has he!" She turned her blue eyes on Daddy and smacked his arm. "Dale! For shame! The poor child is quite obviously shocked beyond belief!"

Daddy chuckled and leaned across the table to bump Taysia's chin. "It's not fly-catching season, honey."

Taysia grabbed up her ice water and gulped several mouthfuls. "I'm sorry, I just—" What did one say in a situation like this? *I'm so glad it's you and not Alzheimer's* just didn't quite seem like the socially correct thing to say. "Well." She took another swallow of icy reality. "This is a surprise, Daddy."

Daddy chuckled as the waiter stepped up to take their order, and it wasn't until she was on her way home later that night that Taysia realized just how much weight had been lifted off her shoulders. It felt a little strange to know Daddy had a girlfriend, but it felt really good to know he wasn't going crazy!

She chuckled as she pulled into her drive and killed the motor. She glanced toward the house.

Kylen, hands clasped behind his head, rocked

easily in her porch swing, the final rays of the setting sun gilding his features.

She closed her eyes, her heart beginning to hammer as though she were in the middle of a tough workout. *What is he doing here?* Wasn't it just this morning that she'd been wishing for some time with him? *I'm crazy to be feeling things for him again!* Well, she couldn't just sit here in the car all night. Quietly she headed for the house.

He grinned as she stepped up onto the porch. "Hi." The word was a soft caress.

"Hi." She adjusted her purse strap. "I got your bouquet." Remembering the words on the card, she flushed and looked down for a moment, then peered back up at him. "It was nice."

He arched his brows, a twinkle in his eyes.

"A lot more than nice. They were beautiful. Thank you." She shuffled her feet.

His face turned serious, and the motion of the swing stopped as he leaned forward, rested his elbows on his knees, and looked intently into her face. "Not half as beautiful as you are," he whispered.

She swallowed and collapsed as casually as she could against the post by her shoulder, pushing down the desire to wrap her arms around him and thank him properly. She did not dare step closer to him. Didn't dare even to look at him. She turned her back to the house and stared out over the street to the golden sunset that was just turning pink along the edges.

She heard him stand, felt him come up beside her. He took her hand.

A tremor raced the length of her spine and back. Still, she did not meet his gaze.

Tugging her over to the swing, he pulled her down beside him. As soon as they were seated, he let go of her hand and tucked his own hands underneath his thighs. He looked over at her. "How was your day?"

She huffed softly, fiddling with a bit of fuzz on her skirt. "Crazy. Strange. Good."

He leaned back to get a better view of her.

She chuckled. "Yeah. All of that. I forgot I was supposed to meet Daddy for breakfast because I was hurrying to the office to see—" Her cheeks flamed. "Well, anyway, he called to remind me and asked me to meet him for dinner."

"Hold on, now." Kylen grinned and bumped her with his shoulder. "You were hurrying to the office to see...what?"

She worried her lower lip, but was unsuccessful at keeping a smile at bay. "You're not playing fair." She met his gaze. "I love getting presents."

His eyes held a smile, but his voice was serious when he said, "Hmmm, I'll have to remember that."

For one heated moment their eyes locked, then Kylen took a visible breath and leaned back. "So you had dinner with your dad tonight. How's the Bungling Burglar doing?"

She chuckled, started to answer, paused, then went ahead and said it, crazy as it sounded and all. "Daddy has a girlfriend."

Kylen arched his brows and folded his arms. "You did have a crazy day."

She nodded. "It does seem a little strange. But I'm so relieved at the same time. I was really worried that he was starting to lose it. But the couple times he's been supposed to meet me and forgot were because he was with his girlfriend. Her name is Loraine."

"So are you okay with it? Not that you have any say in the matter." He grinned.

"At first it felt a little disloyal to Mom. But"—she shrugged—"he deserves to find happiness again. I'm happy for him; at least I will be when I get all the emotional baggage about Mom out of the way."

"Sounds like some exercise therapy is in order. Want to go for a jog?"

She sighed. A jog sounded really good about now. "Sure. Just let me change and I'll be right out."

"First"—he touched her arm to stop her before she stood—"I need to talk to you about Sophia."

She looked at him, holding her breath. She'd known this was coming; she just wasn't sure she was ready for whatever he was about to say. Had Sophia decided to be reasonable? More than likely, not.

"I've met with her a couple of times. She hasn't wanted to meet directly with you, but I've finally talked her into it. She wants to know if we can all get together for lunch next Sunday after church to talk this over."

"Do you think she's going to see reason?"

He shrugged. "One never knows with Sophia."

"Sunday is fine. Where should I meet you?"

"We planned on Fisherman's Wharf."

She shrugged. "Okay, that works for me."

She headed inside to change, hoping Sophia would be sensible for the first time in her life.

Chapter 7

Marie lay back on her couch, hands behind her head as she stared at the familiar water stain on the ceiling. She mashed her lips together and clenched her fists. Her whole body was trembling.

What was she going to do?

Brice was a nice enough guy, maybe. But he certainly didn't seem like a man who—

With a jolt she sat up and hunched forward, her arms curled around her midsection. She rocked forward and back, staring at the bald spot in the carpet between her feet.

She would not cry. She would not cry. She would not cry.

Oh, but this was a fine mess she'd gotten herself into. And there were no easy answers.

She should go talk to Taysia. But the thought of the shock that would be on her face...the disappointment...that held her back. The woman had done so much for her already. She didn't need to be burdened with this.

Her laptop sat on the coffee table, and the website she'd looked up snagged her attention—again. She had *options*, it said. She should list the pros and cons and decide what would make her happy in the future, it said. There were no risks, it said. They could even give her a pill.

Just one little pill.

Her stomach cramped at just the thought, and she scooped her fingers back into her hair and bit her lip. She was unable to stop the tears this time.

Why was she even contemplating this? How had her life choices brought her to this decision? But what would her life be like if she didn't take action?

Her cell phone lay within easy reach. She drew her finger over the screen and swiped in her unlock sequence. The phone number was right there at the top corner of the web page. With a trembling finger, she dialed.

"Family Services Clinic, how may I help you?"

Marie swallowed. "Um...I think I need to make an appointment."

"Certainly. Let me check our schedule."

The woman hadn't even asked why she needed an appointment. Maybe every woman who called for this reason sounded as choked up as she had.

"The soonest I can get you in is on the twenty-eighth at four thirty in the afternoon."

Almost two weeks away? "Uh, yeah, I can make that. Thanks."

She hung up a few minutes later and dropped her phone onto the coffee table, allowing a puff of air to bulge out her cheeks. She could do this. She'd just be her regular self for a few more days. Then she'd take care of this and move on with her life, and no one would be the wiser.

Maybe Brice would be free to hang out later in the week. He might be able to pull her from this melancholy mood.

And even if he couldn't, she would just *act* happy, and then maybe the feelings would follow.

Fake it till you make it—wasn't that what people advised these days?

Taysia gawked at the huge stuffed panda on her porch. She looked around. No one. The morning sun streamed down on a perfectly empty yard. The thing was almost as tall as she was, and it was sitting down! She glanced toward Kylen's house, saw the shutters jostle as a separation between two blinds disappeared, and grinned.

Dropping her gym bag on the porch, she wrestled the beast through her front door and settled it into one of her dining room chairs. It flopped forward, lolling lazily on the tabletop.

"Come on, now. Sit up," she chided, straightening it in the seat. Tucked into the bright red bow tied around its neck was an envelope with her name scrawled on it in Kylen's handwriting. The card was a panda bear chewing on a stalk of bamboo. She grinned and flipped it open. "Do you have room in your heart for one lonely panda bear?" There was no signature, but the handwriting was unmistakable.

She poked the panda in the nose. "No, I do not have room for you." She sighed. "As for the man who sent you? I just might have some room for him." She huffed. "Who am I kidding? I've always had room for him."

Kylen set the twin panda on the top step of Layne's porch and settled into her swing to await her arrival. Grinning, he leaned back and stretched his legs out before him. He hadn't had so much fun in a long time. The look on her face yesterday as she thanked him for the flowers had nearly sent his heart into arrhythmia.

He clasped his hands behind his head. He'd purposely been staying away, giving her time to get used to the idea that he was back in her life. *For good*. But one conversation with her last night and he found he couldn't stay away tonight. He set the swing in motion, closed his eyes, and enjoyed the duet the crickets and gulls sang above the low pulse of the ocean.

A few moments later he heard her turn into the drive. Her little blue car rolled to a stop. Through the windshield he saw her mouth drop open when she caught sight of the panda.

He chuckled and gave the swing another push with his toe.

Blonde hair escaping from her ponytail, she stepped from the car and bent into the backseat to get her things. He wanted to run down the walk and meet her, but he forced himself to stay where he was.

She paused at the bottom of the steps and looked over at him through the porch railings. "I don't have enough room in my little place for another one of these!" The spark of pleasure in her eyes belied the aggravation of her words.

He sauntered over and lifted the huge beast into his arms. Walking back to the swing, he set the panda at one end and seated himself in the middle next to it. "He can sit right here on your swing." He patted the open spot by his side.

Tossing her gym bag by the door, she rolled her lower lip between her teeth, eyeing the small space he'd left for her on the swing.

He scooted a fraction of an inch farther into the panda and thumped the spot again.

Slowly she inched toward him and sat down, plastered like wallpaper to the arm of the swing. Still, their shoulders and knees touched. Gently he set the swing in motion, and they rocked in silence.

Finally she looked over at him. "Thanks for the pandas."

He nodded.

“And the roses. And the coffee and chocolates.” She chuckled.

He grinned. “How about adding ice cream to that list?”

“Ice cream?”

“Come down to Joe’s with me for old times’ sake?” He held his breath.

“Okay, but the panda has to stay here.”

“You got it.” He stood and reached for her hand, pulling her to her feet. Much as he wanted to hang onto her, he let go as soon as they were off the porch, and stuffed his hands deep into his pockets.

Joe’s Ice Cream Truck had been parked at the edge of the beach for so long Kylen seriously doubted if the engine would even turn over anymore. It was an old box truck with the back end converted into a mini ice cream shop. The side of the truck had been retrofitted with a hinged door that, when opened, acted as a roof to keep customers shaded or dry. On sunny days Joe would put out a few small round tables with umbrellas for patrons to sit at.

Kylen cast a sideways glance at Taysia. Coming to Joe’s used to be a daily occurrence for them. He wondered what she was thinking, but her face remained impassive.

As they walked along the path, the bottom half of the sun slid past the black line of ocean horizon, painting the smooth surface of the water a bright shade of orange. Soft cirrus clouds wisped across the sky, reflecting the orange sunset in peach hues. The soft swish of ocean waves pulsed against the shore, and somewhere a bullfrog croaked out a tympanic rhythm.

Kylen swallowed hard and fisted the lining of his pockets into his tight grip, because with all the beauty surrounding him, he still was having a hard time keeping his eyes off the woman at his side. What would he do if she never came to a place where she could trust him again? He didn't want to think on that. The consequences of that were too painful to even contemplate. He wanted to spend every minute of the rest of his life knowing this woman by his side was his to cherish. *Lord, give me patience.*

Taysia wrapped both hands around her upper arms and rubbed away the gooseflesh. The chill bumps had nothing to do with being cold. The weather was warm and balmy, but the man walking next to her had gotten under her skin. She longed to reach out and slide her arm through his. But there was Blaine to think of. If she were going to allow this thing with Kylen to go on, she really needed to have a serious talk with Blaine.

Joe glanced up from inside the truck. Over his shoulder a bare bulb hung from the ceiling, several moths banging their heads in a mad flutter against it. A bright smile parted Joe's face as he saw who was approaching. "Hey! It's been a few years since you two used to come down here!" He placed one hand flat against his chest. "It does this ol' heart good to see you together again!"

Taysia grinned, suddenly feeling shy. Yes, she really needed to have that talk with Blaine before he heard it from some town gossip.

Kylen stretched his hand through the opening in the side of the truck. "Joe, good to see you again. I tell you, I've been craving one of your special Coffee Caramel Chocolate Thunder Bars for a long time."

Taysia's mouth watered simply at the mention of Joe's signature treat.

Joe laughed. "That's what keeps people coming back, Kylen. And it's just what I like to hear! One Triple C&T coming right up!"

"Make that two, Joe." Taysia dug for the five-dollar bill she'd tucked into her back pocket, but Kylen caught her hand as she reached to give it to Joe and paid with his own money. He grinned at her and folded her five back into her palm.

Ice cream in hand, they meandered down the beach until they found a driftwood log to sink down onto. Taysia kicked aside her flip-flops and sank her toes into the warmth of the sand.

Kylen bumped her with his shoulder. "Thanks for coming down here with me."

She glanced up at him and grinned. He had chocolate at the corner of his mouth. Before she realized what she was doing, she reached up to rub it away. Time paused in the electric jolt of the moment, and she studied him without reservation for the first time since he'd come home.

The stubble under her fingers was rough, much rougher than the last time she'd had occasion to touch Kylen's face. A few more lines etched the corners of his eyes. His eyebrows were bushier. A new scar—a thin white line—disappeared into the hair at his temple, and there was an indent in his earlobe where the hole had closed up.

A small smile tilted the corner of Kylen's mouth, and one eyebrow lifted slightly. "I can think of a better way to get that off of there...I'm just saying." His second brow joined its mate.

Realizing her hand still rested at the corner of his mouth, Taysia snatched it into her lap. Her cheeks heated, and she turned to study the coral hues painting the sky. "Y-you got rid of your earring."

"Mmm-hmm." He chomped a bite off the corner of his bar.

Was that a little disappointment she heard in his tone? She suppressed a smile and savored a mouthful of perfection on a stick.

"I was part of an undercover operation in Seattle, so the earring had to go."

Her heart jolted at the word. "Undercover?" she asked.

He nodded, then grinned at her. "I was posing as a librarian. My captain didn't think the earring fit the profile. Then after that assignment was over, it just never…" He shrugged.

Taysia leaned back. "You went undercover as a *librarian*?"

His face turned deadly serious. "That's a highly dangerous position, I want you to know!"

She giggled. "It is, huh?"

"Infected paper cuts are a leading cause of death among librarians." He held his finger and thumb a scant quarter inch apart. "I was this close to death. Every. Single. Day."

Taysia arched her brow and whispered, "Sounds dangerous!"

"Mmmm, very."

"What in the world were you doing undercover as a librarian?"

He leaned closer and lowered his voice, holding up his fingers again. "This close. To death. Every day."

She laughed outright. She'd forgotten how Kylen could turn the most mundane subjects into humorous conversations.

He threw his hands up in the air and angled her a look of mock hurt. "When a man risks his life for his country, you'd think he'd get a little respect."

"You're right." She jabbed him with her elbow. "Just the other day I was watching *America's Most Wanted*, and they were telling about this terrible killer who murdered all his victims with paper cuts!"

He chuckled. Then winced. "Ouch!"

Taysia grimaced. "Yeah. That would be a terrible way to go, wouldn't it? I can't believe I said that." She crinkled her toes and pressed them deeper into the sand. "So, seriously, what were you doing undercover at a library?"

"There was a bomb threat. A man mailed a letter to the library threatening to blow the place up because they'd revoked his library card. I was part of a team assigned to make sure he didn't get the chance to follow through on his threats."

"Whoa. Talk about your disgruntled book lover!"

Kylen chuckled. "Yeah."

"So did you catch him?"

"He got caught, but not at the library. He was pulled over in a routine traffic stop in what we can only guess was his trip to the library. He stepped out of his car waving a gun, and the officer shot him. Later when they searched his car, they did find a bomb inside a backpack in the trunk."

"Oh my goodness! I remember that. That was just a year or so ago! It was all over the news."

He nodded.

"Wow!" She leaned over and bumped him with her shoulder. "You do deserve a lot of respect."

"I know!" The wink he tossed her belied the arrogance of the statement, and she chuckled.

A gull shrilled a cry as it glided across the

purple of the evening sky, drawing their attention to the sunset once more. The corals and peaches had deepened to stark orange edged with crimson and shot through with a turquoise streak so vivid no one would believe the sight if an artist painted it on a canvas.

"Beautiful," Taysia whispered.

"Yeah." The last of his ice cream disappeared in one bite, and Kylen leaned both arms on his knees. For a long time they simply sat in companionable silence and watched God's palette change and fade.

Finally, Kylen stood, dusted the sand off his shorts, and reached out a hand.

She took it without thinking, and he pulled her to her feet.

Her face was now mere inches from the molten intensity in his dark eyes.

She swallowed. The desire bursting to life inside her cemented her to the spot.

His eyes never leaving hers, he slid a warm caress across her palm until their fingers interlaced. Dipping his chin down, he studied her, as though looking to see if she would object.

Her heart pounded like waves in a windstorm, and she closed her eyes as though that could press down the surge of trembling overtaking her. She should object. But the words would not form.

He tightened his grip and trailed the fingers of his free hand across her cheek. "Layne, I promise not to hurt you, hon."

She looked at him again and, for the first time since he'd come home, felt the defensive walls she'd put up begin to crumble.

His gaze dropped to her mouth even as he tucked her closer, with their intertwined fingers resting at the small of her back. Slowly his head dipped down toward her.

Taysia felt sure her heart would flop out of her chest and land in the sand at any moment. She couldn't believe she was letting down her guard for him again. Yet, she was powerless to move. Powerless to step away. In fact, as if drawn by a magnetic pull, she rose up on her tiptoes to meet him halfway, one hand reaching out to rest against his chest.

He froze and touched her chin to stop her forward momentum, his lips a mere breath away. His voice a rough whisper, he said, "Tell me now if this isn't something you are ready for."

I'm a fool! Her breath rushed out in a small puff as she released his hand and wrapped her arms around his neck. The fraction of space that separated them dissipated with a small tilt of her head, and she gave herself fully to the kiss.

He kissed her slowly, gently. But the tremble that coursed through his arms revealed the measure of his feelings. Taysia's hands curled into the hair at the back of his head as the kiss intensified, and she pressed herself closer, relishing the feel of his arms around her and the sweet chocolaty taste of him.

"Taysia." He breathed her name as his lips trailed a hot path to her earlobe.

A shiver of pleasure rippled through her, and she tipped her chin to accept his kisses on her throat.

With a sudden jagged growl, Kylen grabbed her upper arms and set her from him.

She blinked.

His chest heaved in quick bursts.

The cadence of her own breathing matched his, and confusion fogged her thinking. Her eyes focused on his mouth, suddenly wanting more than anything to feel his lips pressed to hers again. She leaned toward him.

He snatched his hands from her arms and jumped back.

Eyes widening, she lurched a step to catch her balance.

He scrubbed his fingers through his hair and paced away. Without turning to look at her, he said, "We need to get back."

Disappointment washed over her. What had she done to change his mood so quickly? She'd never kissed anyone but Kylen—well, unless she counted the chicken peck that Blaine had given her the other night, but that was like comparing a drippy faucet to Niagara Falls. Was her kissing really that awful? The thought hit her like a slap in the face, and her cheeks heated.

He waited in silence, staring out toward the horizon, while she fumbled for her flip-flops in the sand and gathered up both their ice cream sticks.

The walk back to her house was long, silent, and miserable. She berated herself for the fool she was. Hadn't she just told herself a few days ago that she wasn't the kind of girl who could keep Kylen's attention?

When they turned up the street toward their houses, Kylen reached out and laced his fingers through hers.

Talk about mixed signals!

She tried to pull her hand away, but Kylen tightened his grip with a gentle squeeze. "It's not you, Layne."

She pondered those words the rest of the way up the street, feeling like she'd taken a ride on an emotional cyclone.

Her house lay shrouded in darkness. She'd forgotten to turn the porch light on.

They paused as if by mutual agreement at the foot of her stairs.

"Kylen, I—"

"Layne, I'm—"

They both paused, waiting for the other.

Finally Kylen chuckled and stepped toward her. "Layne, I'm sorry. I just..." He leaned forward and kissed her, a quick kiss that nonetheless sent her pulse skittering. "I need to explain."

She released his hand and folded her arms. "It's okay. You don't have to—"

"No." He fingered her hair. "I have a feeling

that I do. It wasn't—I just—you make me feel things that—"

From the darkness on her porch, the chains holding up the swing squeaked as someone stood and cleared his throat.

Taysia's heart lurched with dread even as she and Kylen both spun toward the sound. She already knew who it would be, and she wished he hadn't had to find out about her and Kylen this way.

Her fears were confirmed when Blaine leaned over the rail, the moonlight just bright enough to reveal his narrowed eyes and clenched jaw. "Hope I'm not interrupting anything?"

"Blaine!" Taysia suddenly felt light headed.

Blaine thrust his hands deep into the pockets of his slacks. "In the flesh. You weren't expecting me, I see."

"I was just leaving." Kylen reached out and touched her hand, pitching his voice low so Blaine wouldn't hear. "I have to work the early shift tomorrow. But I'll drop by Mom's Gym as soon as I can. I want to talk to you about tonight. I'll go home so you can talk to him. Please don't worry about tonight. It wasn't anything you did."

"You're sure?"

He chuckled softly. "Heaven help me. Yes, I'm sure." Tapping her on the nose, he stepped back. "See you tomorrow."

"O-okay." She watched him go, elation at his words elevating her heart rate, but dreading the talk she knew she needed to have with Blaine and still wondering what had caused Kylen to pull away so suddenly. She sighed. If confusion were fuel, she'd be able to supply enough for a space shuttle launch.

She tentatively climbed the steps and leaned on the rail next to Blaine, looking out into the darkness. "Where's your car?"

"I left it at the church and walked over."

"Oh..." Guilt clenched a fist around her heart. She should have told him a week ago that she was starting to have feelings for Kylen again. "We need to talk."

He huffed. "You think?"

Taysia couldn't meet his gaze. Instead, she studied the swaying shadows of her weeping willow tree. "Kylen and I...we—"

"Hasn't he broken your heart enough times already?" Blaine put his back to the rail and jangled the coins in his pocket.

That was true enough to obliterate any defense she might make. Taysia folded her arms and clenched her hands tight. Pressing her lips together, she held her silence. She wasn't quite sure how to respond to that. Kylen had broken her heart. More than once. Something her grandma used to say came to mind. *Burn me once, shame on you. Burn me twice, shame on me.* Yet, here she was going back for perhaps a third roasting. Did that make her a pathological pyro-masochist? She suppressed a groan. Truth to tell,

Blaine was much safer all around. *Safer and…boring.*

Somewhere in the bushes a bullfrog trilled a long, deep croak, and a soft breeze swayed the fronds of the weeping willow.

What could she tell him that would let him down easy?

Chink. Chink. Chink. Blaine kept torturing the change in his pocket.

Finally she glanced over at him. "I'm sorry, Blaine. I just…need to see where this goes."

"Well"—his voice trembled as he clomped down the steps and paused on the path—"you know where to find me when you realize he's no good for you."

Taysia dropped her head onto her arms and waited until the crunch of his footsteps in the gravel dissipated. Then she allowed the groan that had been building inside of her to escape. "God, please don't let that happen!"

Chapter 8

Marie was late for work.

Taysia did her best to suppress a growl as she pawed through the stacks of papers on Marie's desk, but she was afraid it might have slipped out. A surreptitious peek at the blubbering new client across from her confirmed she was still an emotional basket case. Another lady waited patiently, and thankfully dry-eyed, off to one side. *Where in the world has Marie moved those forms to?*

The newly pregnant enrollee across the desk dabbed at her eyes again and prattled on about how she didn't want to look as flabby as her sister had after delivering her first baby.

Taysia pushed the box of tissues closer to her and angled a subtle glance at the large clock on the wall. She'd had to cancel her Third Trimester Toning class in order to run the front desk, and unless Marie showed up soon, she might have to do the same with her next class, as well—which meant refunding a portion of the clients' payments.

She finally found the forms she needed under a stack of brochures. "Here they are." *About time!* She handed each of them a pen and did her best to smile, hoping it didn't look as plastic as it felt.

Just then the front doors opened and Marie floated in on cloud nine with all the air of an angel in an ice cream commercial—complete with sugar cone and chocolate scoop.

Taysia, took a deep breath and clenched her teeth tight to prevent the rant that begged to burst forth. She looked pointedly at the large wall clock and then back to Marie, her fists planted firmly on her hips. As Marie sauntered through the lobby, Taysia caught her own reflection in the large mirror across the room. The receipts and brochures clenched in her hands splayed out like the ruffled tail feathers of an angry hen. With a huff she plunked them down onto the desk.

Marie gave an airy sigh and bent to shove her purse into the drawer. A large blob of brown ice cream landed with a splat on the pile of papers Taysia had just tossed down. Ignoring Taysia's glare, Marie turned instead to the customer, who had taken one look at the form and burst out crying in earnest.

"What's the matter, hon?"

"You need to know my pre-pregnancy weight? What? Is this some sort of a last farewell ceremony? Roxy told me never to expect to see it again!" She snatched another tissue from the box and blew her nose loudly.

Marie peered over at Taysia and mouthed, "Roxy?"

"Pudgy sister," Taysia mouthed back, sketching a large, round gesture in the air.

Marie's eyes widened in understanding. "There now, honey. Don't you worry about a thing. Miss Green is the best!" She nodded her head in Taysia's direction. "You'll feel like you hired your own personal trainer by the time she gets you into shape, and there's no worry about you ending up looking like your pudgy sister, okay? Why don't you go on over to the sign-up board and see if any of those classes look like they'd fit into your schedule. Don't forget, you want to sign up for First Trimester Fitness, alright?" Marie quick-licked a drip before it could join its mate on the desktop.

"Okay. Thank you."

With a hasty glance around to make sure no one else needed her attention, Marie rolled her eyes in heavenly ecstasy, flopped back into the desk chair, and stretched her long legs out before her. "You should have *seen* him today, Taysia! He's so *gorgeous*! Sorry I'm late, by the way, but I just couldn't pull myself away. He looked into my eyes and asked me if I had any pets! Can you believe it? I mean, a guy doesn't ask if you have any pets if he's not at least a little interested, don't you think? He's..."

She paused to lick her cone, and Taysia inserted, "Who in the world are you talking about?"

"Brice, the-hot-guy-from-Sunday-and-he-took-me-to-Joe's-Ice-Cream-Truck-down-at-the-beach-he's-so-gorgeous!" Her words ran together in high-pitched excitement.

Taysia had the distinct feeling Marie was making herself out to be just a tad more excited than she really was. "Marie, I couldn't help but notice on Sunday that you and Reece still have feelings for each other."

Marie's jaw jutted off to one side. "Reece made it perfectly clear that I'm not good enough for him when he broke up with me. There is nothing between Reece and me anymore."

"Whatever he said, Marie, I'm sure he didn't mean it the way it came across to you."

"It doesn't matter. It's over." Marie blinked hard, and then it was like a mask dropped over her features. She looked from the cone in her hand to her perfectly toned figure. "Oh! This thing is going to add five pounds, but it was worth every crunch I'll have to do! Brice's so *hot*!"

Taysia pressed the day's schedule into Marie's non-ice-cream-cone-occupied hand and gave her what she hoped was an understanding smile. "I might have known it was something important that made you late. Now I've got a class to—"

The front doors opened, and Kylen strode in wearing his blue uniform.

The epaulets emphasized the width of his shoulders, and the gun belt around his waist drew her gaze to his slim hips. It took a moment before she realized her mouth had gaped open and Kylen was grinning at her like a dog with a meaty bone.

Marie doodled her tongue across her ice cream and cocked her head, glancing back and forth between them.

Taysia waved her hand to ward off the questions she could see coming. "Hi, Kylen. Give me a second, would you?"

"Sure." He sauntered to one end of the desk and picked up a copy of *Today's Baby*, flipping through it.

Suppressing a grin, Taysia stepped over to glance at a clipboard on the desk and told Marie, "Let's make sure that the ladies from Third Trimester Toning get a refund for the canceled class today."

"Okay." Marie at least had the grace to look guilty, so Taysia decided to leave off chastising her for being late this time.

"Did anyone call to say they wouldn't be here for Second Trimester Stretches today?"

Marie gave a little sigh of relief and slurped another lick. "Nope. You should have all five today." She lowered her voice. "So what gives with you and Mr. Dreamy?"

Taysia ignored her. "Oh, good. I'm glad Francine will be here today. She's missed quite a few classes lately."

"Must be hard, being a single mom." Marie's voice dropped again. "So is he making moves? I mean, I don't think I've ever seen a guy look at you that way before."

Taysia grabbed the article on nutrition that she wanted to hand out at the end of her next class and prayed her cheeks didn't look as red as they felt. "Keep your mind on your work, Marie."

Walking back to the copier, she could feel the burn of Kylen's gaze and Marie's curious scrutiny. She kept her back to them and finished making her copies.

The room was strangely silent.

Finally Taysia grabbed her papers, turned, and met Kylen's glance. His dark eyes were soft and warm. Blast her disobedient heart. It was beating like she'd just jogged a mile instead of made five copies on a copier. And she couldn't seem to look away. One of his eyes closed in a quick wink.

Marie inspected the two of them as she chomped down the last of her cone. "Taysia, I do believe you—"

"Marie, would you please make sure all the mats are set up for me in the classroom?" Taysia tore her attention away from Kylen long enough to give Marie a pointed look.

Marie rose with a knowing arch of her eyebrows and in a stage whisper said, "Don't let him get away, Tays. He's much better looking than Blaine." Blue eyes twinkling, she sashayed from the lobby with a parting "Y'all be good now!"

Kylen's mouth quirked. "Where did you find her?"

Taysia smiled. "I hired her through a youth mentoring program. She's basically raised herself since she was thirteen, when her mom walked out on them. Last year, after her father was arrested, she came in looking for work. I figured maybe I could do some good for her. She's come a long way since then. Grown up a lot." She sighed. "We still have a ways to go."

Kylen's face turned suddenly serious. "That's great, Layne. She couldn't have a better mentor."

Taysia swallowed. "Thanks."

He cleared his throat and scuffed one foot against the carpet. "How did your talk with Blaine go?"

"Well..." She cocked her head. "It went alright, considering."

"So you and I...we're still...?" He looked away and muttered something low under his breath.

Hardly able to believe his nervous actions, Taysia suppressed a grin and waited.

Rolling his lips together, he glanced back over at her, then stilled. His eyes narrowed. "You are enjoying this just a little too much."

She giggled and took pity on him. "I told Blaine that I wanted to see where this thing between us would go."

His shoulders relaxed. "You did?"

She nodded.

Kylen glanced across the lobby at the two women still filling out papers and stepped closer to her. "About last night..."

Her heart threatened to stop.

"Layne, I just want to be really careful not to lose you, again. And I certainly don't want to cross any lines we shouldn't cross until...well...yet. Kissing you like that, I could easily..." His gaze bored into hers, and he stroked a soft caress against her cheek. "I was just stepping back before things got out of control."

She felt the crimson flood that stained her cheeks.

Kylen grinned and stepped even closer, taking her hand and toying with her fingers. "You know, I'm sure there is a law on the books somewhere that prohibits the way I feel just when you look at me that way."

Wow. What did a girl say to something like that? Nothing came to mind, so she just stared at him in sloppy-grinned silence.

As the moment stretched, he chuckled nervously. "That was kind of corny, huh?"

"N-no." She paused. Then smiled mischievously. "Well, probably, but I liked it. I'm just glad it wasn't something I did. I was worried that I'd—" *Blast!* Her cheeks blazed again.

"Trust me. You have nothing to worry about."

"Oh, good." *Lame, that was really lame*. She rolled the nutrition papers into a tube and tapped them against her palm. "I really need to get to class, so I'll talk to you later?" Walking backward, she started toward the door to her classroom.

"When's a good time?"

Glancing over her shoulder to make sure her path was clear, she looked back at him. "How about tomorrow?"

His mouth tipped. "How about tonight? I have an idea for a little road trip. Can you go on an overnighter—we'll be back by tomorrow evening?"

She raised her brow.

"Separate rooms, I promise."

Tomorrow was Saturday—nothing going on. "Where are we going?"

"My secret. Is that a yes?"

She cocked her head and then nodded in consent.

"It's going to be fun, I promise." He grinned and waggled his eyebrows. "I'm looking forward to it."

Her heart lurched. "Me too." She spun around to escape the magnetic draw of his warm gaze and crashed into the doorframe with a loud crack that drew the eyes of all her students and Marie to the back of the room. Hissing as the pain hit her with full force, Taysia clutched the doorframe and waited for her head to clear.

Kylen was at her side in an instant. He assessed her quickly and, seeing that she was alright, said, "There's a door there. Careful you don't crash into it."

She glowered at him good-naturedly.

"You okay?" he tried.

Taysia didn't reply except to nod once. What was there to say? She was fine. Just humiliated that he'd seen her idiocy once again.

He leaned forward. "I'd kiss it better, but I think we have an audience."

She punched his arm. "Go. I'll see you tonight."

In Kylen's convertible headed north on I-5, Taysia leaned her head back and relished the feel of the wind whipping through her hair. She angled her head on the headrest and studied Kylen's profile. He'd changed out of his uniform into his customary cargo shorts and T-shirt, blue this time. Dark sunglasses hid his eyes, but emphasized the angular line of his stubbled jaw, and made her want to reach out and rub her fingers across it. She tucked her hand under her leg so she wouldn't be tempted to follow through on the action. His dark curls frolicked at the whim of the wind, and his hand, resting casually on the stick shift, begged for her to hold it. She pushed her hand a little farther under her leg.

He hadn't told her where they were going yet. Just "north" and "bring layers because we'll be outside and you never know what the weather is going to be like up there."

He glanced over and reached up to touch the knot on her forehead with a gentle finger. "You really gave yourself a good knock there."

"Mmm-hmm."

Gently, he tugged her hand toward him, sliding his fingers between hers. She tried to ignore the warm feeling wrapping around her heart but failed miserably. Especially when his thumb caressed a slow, methodical path over the pulse point at her wrist.

She closed her eyes. *Lord, don't let me fall too hard for him if nothing is going to come of it. Not again.*

The tone of the tires on the pavement changed, and Taysia opened her eyes. She glanced around in confusion, stretching tautness from her muscles. The car's top was up, and it was fully dark. Kylen pulled to a stop in front of a Best Western, its blue-and-yellow sign reflecting off a puddle in the parking spot next to them.

Taysia glanced at Kylen, her confusion apparently evident on her face.

He grinned. "You fell asleep. And we're here."

She rubbed her eyes. "Here, where?"

"Seattle." He killed the engine.

"Wow." She stifled a yawn. "I must have slept for a long time."

"Couple of hours."

"I'm sorry." She rubbed her face, hoping she hadn't drooled all over his leather seats.

"Don't be." He glanced out the windshield. "I

thought I'd get us a couple rooms, then we could get some dinner. Sound good?"

"I'm starved!"

He chuckled. "Good. Me too."

A thought hit her and she blurted, "Kylen, I didn't bring any formal clothes."

His brow lowered in a thoughtful frown.

Immediately realizing how presumptuous she'd sounded, her face heated. "I didn't mean for that to sound like—"

He laid a finger across her lips and leaned toward her. "I didn't plan for anything too fancy on this trip. I'm sorry, I didn't think of it."

"That's fine. I'm sorry, I didn't mean—"

Another touch stopped her. This time he grinned. "Don't worry about it. Let's just go inside."

She pressed her lips together and nodded. Why did she feel so poised and controlled when she was with Blaine and so...*not* around Kylen?

Inside, Kylen secured them each a room, and soon they were back in the car and on the road again.

He glanced over at her. "I know of this great little restaurant that offers casual dining but has some great atmosphere. Sound okay?"

"Sure." Anything sounded fine, as long as she got to go there with the man by her side, and that was what scared her. Because as hard as she had tried to keep her heart safe from Kylen's charms, she had come full circle and fallen for him again.

The Rainforest Café was everything its name promised it would be. A small gift shop filled with all kinds of jungle critters, both stuffed and collectible, filled the restaurant entrance and was separated from the dining area by huge saltwater fish tanks. The fish darted and swayed in colorful abandon, the thrum of their filtration systems a low, peaceful gurgle.

Taysia took in the restaurant with gaping mouth as she followed Kylen and the waitress back to their table. Every inch of the ceiling sprouted branches, leaves, vines, or some sort of flora. Two central posts looked like trees growing right up through the middle of the room—and vines and flowers grew on and around them, as well. Around the perimeter of the room, several groups of animals clustered, from gorillas on one end to elephants on the other. Bright splashes of color in the jungle canopy revealed parrots, seemingly ready to take flight. Mood music that Taysia would label *Jungle Animal Chatter* played from hidden speakers throughout the room, and along one back wall a wide waterfall cascaded into a shimmering pool, a light mist drifting up from the base.

Their table sat toward the back of the room, right next to a display of a mother elephant and her baby.

"That is huge!" Taysia eyed the animals.

While only half of the mother elephant protruded from the wall, the beast was well over twice her height, and she couldn't imagine ever meeting one of those in the wild.

The waitress, dressed in a khaki safari uniform, grinned as she dropped their menus on the table. "This is one of my favorite displays. Y'all get settled in. I'll be right back with some water and to see about your drink order."

Taysia was halfway down into the chair Kylen had pulled out for her when the mother elephant tipped back its head, raised its trunk, and blasted a call across the room. Taysia squawked like a shot duck and leaped back, tripping over the chair and sprawling into Kylen.

With a bark of laughter, he wrapped his arms tightly around her and pulled her firmly back against him.

"Did I forget to mention that the animals move and make noise?" He pressed a kiss to her jaw, just below her ear, but she could still feel the tremor of laughter coursing through him.

The adrenaline rush left as quickly as it had come and took with it the strength from her legs. She smacked his arm in humiliation as she noticed two businessmen at the next table laughing at her. "Yes, you did."

"Well"—he tucked her closer and nuzzled her neck—"I can't honestly say that I'm sorry."

She grinned and gave him an elbow to the ribs as she stepped away. Her face was warm enough to cook the elephant, which once again stood placidly still and innocent looking. She sank into her chair and hid behind the large menu.

For the rest of the night, every fifteen minutes or so when the elephant trumpeted its preprogrammed duty, Kylen busted up laughing. And, when the meal wound down, he wouldn't let her leave until she had chosen a cute, cuddly elephant from the gift shop as a reminder of the trip.

It was late when they stopped in front of her hotel room door.

Taysia couldn't remember the last time she'd had an evening filled with so much fun. "I had a really good time tonight, Kylen. Thanks." She fingered the soft ear of the stuffed toy.

He grinned and jotted something on an imaginary paper. "Taysia finds scary elephants fun."

A laugh burst out rather loudly, especially for a hotel hallway this late at night. Hunching her shoulders guiltily, she covered her mouth, then whispered, "You're not going to let me live this one down, are you?"

There was a twinkle in his warm gaze as he stepped closer. He cocked his head, squinched up his eyes, and studied the ceiling as though deep in thought. "Mmmm...probably not."

She whacked him with the elephant. "Well, then—" Presenting him with her back, she slid her key card into the lock. "No good-night kiss for you!"

But before she could open the door and make

her escape, Kylen had her by the waist. "Whoa. Whoa." He turned a half circle and set her out into the hallway, then planted himself in her doorway with his arms folded. "I *might* be talked into reconsidering."

"Oh? So you want to take this to the negotiating table, do you?"

"I do."

She giggled and sauntered closer, tapping the stuffed elephant against her palm and suddenly finding it a little hard to breathe. "So? What terms, dear sir?"

"Well…" He cupped his chin and studied her with a mischievous smirk. "I'm thinking that for a good-night kiss, I might be talked into forgetting the Great Elephant Incident." He plucked the stuffed animal from her grasp and dropped it on the floor by their feet.

Her eyes narrowed. "Forgetting for how long?"

The grin that spread across his face told her he had her right where he wanted her. And when he forked his fingers into her hair, she knew she was right where *she* wanted to be.

"That all depends on how amazing the kiss is." The words emerged on a gruff rumble, and his gaze dropped to her mouth for a moment before rebounding.

"Well"—her chest tightened with anticipation as she slipped her arms around his back and kissed him softly—"let's see how much I can make you forget." Her lips skimmed like silk across his for a moment, and then she pulled back. "How's that?"

"Mmmm." He wrapped one arm behind her and tucked her closer. "That was a good start...but I still have this vivid picture of you leaping into my arms because of a little animatronic elephant."

"Vivid is not good."

He angled his head as though thinking about it. "It is fading a little. Give it another try."

She laughed outright and kissed him again, her arms moving of their own volition to wrap around his neck. This time when he pulled away, they were both breathing hard.

Resting his forehead against hers, he inhaled a long draw of air. "Who am I and why am I here kissing you?"

She chuckled. "That good, huh?"

"Mmmm." He dropped a slow kiss on first one corner of her mouth, then the other. Looking deep into her eyes, he spoke softly. "I love you, Layne."

She swallowed. She wanted to reply that she loved him too, but she couldn't get the words to move past her suddenly closed-off throat. Feeling helpless, she pulled back slightly and studied the sleeve of his T-shirt.

"Don't worry about it." He pressed a kiss to the top of her head, then stepped away and bent to retrieve the elephant. "This is going to take a while, I know, Layne. I don't want you to feel rushed. Just take your time. I'm not going anywhere." Handing her the elephant, he added, "See you bright and early tomorrow? I know this awesome breakfast place."

Taysia couldn't push back a feeling of deflation. And she could hear the edge of hurt in his voice. They'd had such a nice evening, and now she had ruined it. What was holding her back? She honestly believed Kylen had changed. So why couldn't she seem to tell him that?

Folding her arms, she asked, "How early?"

"Seven?"

"Okay. Sounds fine." She smiled wistfully. "I'm sorry, Ky. I'm trying. I really believe you've changed, I just..." She shrugged. "I don't know."

"We'll get through this, Layne. Have a good night."

Even though he was trying to encourage her, defeat traced the edges of his tone. And when his door clicked shut, Taysia felt it like a jab to the heart. Could they really get through this? Would she ever be able to trust this man again?

She flopped down onto the bed fully clothed and stared up at the ceiling. "God..." The word just hung there in the stillness for a long time. "I don't know what to say. Why can't I seem to let go of the past and move on with Kylen? I think I love him. And I know I hurt him tonight with my silence, but I'm just so afraid of him hurting me again."

She stilled. There it was again. Her blasted

pride. All wrapped up in its own prickly little coat of armor and blocking all attempts at letting go of the hurt.

And where would she be, if she opened herself up to Kylen and he walked away from her again? Right back where she'd been when he came back to town. And that hadn't been such a bad place.

But where would she be if she trusted him again and things worked out this time? A genuine smile bloomed on her face. Now, that would be a place she'd like to visit.

"God, please help me conquer my pride. Don't let me think on past hurts. Don't let me worry about getting hurt again. Just help me to look to the future."

Chapter 9

Kylen knocked on her door at the promised early hour the next morning and handed her a steaming cup of her favorite Starbucks.

"Mmmm, thanks." She trundled her bag out and let the door shut behind her as she took the first wake-me-up sip. Her breath released in pure satisfaction.

Kylen chuckled as he took the case from her and led the way down the hall. "I already checked us out."

"Oh, good! Breakfast!" Taysia actually gave a little skip as she hurried around to her side of the car. She couldn't remember the last time she'd felt this lighthearted.

He laughed outright. "What do you want?"

"Anywhere's fine, I'm famished!"

Kylen sank into the driver's seat and angled her a look. "That's good, because I know a place that is known for its huge servings and great food. I've been craving some of their biscuits and gravy since I moved back home."

"That good, huh?"

He nodded. "That good."

But when they'd been driving for more than twenty minutes, Taysia began to get curious. "Where are we going?"

"You'll see." He reached over and laced his fingers with hers. "I had to pick someplace faraway, because I knew it would take me a bit to work up the courage to hold your hand." He tossed her a wink.

She huffed. "Yeah, right."

"You don't believe me?" he asked as he pulled into a left-turn lane.

"You've never had to work up courage to do anything in your life, Ky. You just do it."

"Ah, well, there you are wrong. You are very scary. I've had to work up my courage to talk to you lots of times." He grinned.

She chuckled and mimicked fangs hanging over her lower lip.

He nodded. "Yeah. A lot like that."

She smacked his arm, then glanced out the window. "Kylen, there's nothing out here. Where are we going? We're in the middle of nowhere."

"There's where you are wrong. We're here." He turned right into a dusty gravel parking lot next to what looked like an old school and a bowling alley.

Taysia scrunched up her nose as dust filtered up from under their tires. A sign proclaiming "The Maltby Café" hung weathered and forlorn off the corner of the old bowling alley. An old bowling pin replica still hung on the front of the brick façade. Taysia peered out at the building, but didn't undo her seatbelt.

"Are you sure we're in the right place?"

Kylen grinned and pressed the release on her clasp. "Yep."

Reluctantly, she got out of the car and followed him across the tightly packed parking lot toward the building. There sure were a lot of cars out here in the middle of nowhere. Standing around the gravel parking lot, clusters of people chatted with one another. And a loudspeaker wired to the wall above the door squawked, "Stevens, party of four...Stevens, party of four, your table is ready!"

Taysia wrinkled her brow at the old silver cone-shaped speaker. "The Maltby Café looks like it needs to enter into the twenty-first century."

Kylen chuckled. "It doesn't look like much, but you just wait. See all these people? They are waiting for tables." He pulled open the door at the corner of the building and stepped aside so she could precede him.

A narrow set of stairs descended down to

another door. This place wasn't just in a bowling alley, it was in the *basement* of the bowling alley. *Great, just my luck! And I'm so hungry! They probably only offer greasy doughnuts and black coffee. Cop fare.*

She pulled open the door at the foot of the stairs and jolted to a stop. The waiting area was jammed with people, wall to wall. A woman smiled at her and pressed herself as close to the wall as she could to let them in.

Kylen and Taysia managed to squeeze inside and find seats on the padded bench against the wall by the cash register. As they waited for their names to be called, Taysia scanned the little basement room. The walls were plastered with grassy-looking stucco in a warm yellow. Dark green beams lined the low ceiling, and several large plants graced the corners of the room. She was pleasantly surprised by the inviting atmosphere. *Okay, maybe they at least have cream with their coffee.*

A man and his wife were called to follow the waitress, and as they moved out of the waiting area, a shelving unit caught Taysia's eye. In crystal-clear to-go containers, cinnamon rolls the size of dinner plates tempted patrons both coming and going.

Taysia's mouth watered at the sight. She leaned toward Kylen. "Those look delicious!"

He grinned. "Yep. The food here is great. I've never had something here that I didn't like."

Taysia ordered Swedish pancakes filled with strawberries and topped with a huge dollop of crème fraîche. She actually rolled her eyes in ecstasy at her first bite. "Mmmm." The food really did live up to his praise.

Kylen nodded and stuffed a huge bite of biscuit and gravy into his mouth.

"So where are we going today?"

A twinkle leapt into his eyes. "Well, I had plans just to drive around the city, maybe visit Pike Place Market. And I'm thinking a trip to the zoo is in order."

"Oh! The zoo sounds fun."

He nodded. "Yeah. I hear the Woodland Park Zoo has a great elephant exhibit."

With a good-natured growl, Taysia wadded up her napkin and chucked it at him. "What happened to 'Who am I and why am I here kissing you?'"

He tossed her a wink. "Memory is a funny thing. It comes and goes."

She laughed. "I'll have to remember that." She angled him a warning glance. "Don't think it won't come back to haunt you!"

He gave her an unrepentant grin and stuffed another bite in his mouth. For a time they ate in silence, just enjoying the good food and each other's company.

Finally Kylen finished his last bite and pushed his plate aside. "So"—his face turned serious—"tell me what you'd like to do with your future.

What plans do you have for Mom's Gym?" He leaned on the table and gave her his full attention.

She mulled that over as she finished a bite. "Well, assuming I get past this lawsuit with Sophia, I've been wanting to add a class for teens about pregnancy awareness. Maybe cover health issues related to abortion, too. I want girls to abstain from having sex until they are married, but if they do mess up and get pregnant..." Her gaze darted to his, and she felt the heat that filled her face.

"Wait—did you...?" Kylen reached across the table and covered her hand.

"No." She shook her head. "But it could have happened."

"I'm so sorry, Layne."

"I know. Me too. We both...well, anyhow, I want girls to know there are more options out there than abortion. And the risks that go along with abortion later down the road."

"That's great, Layne. You could even start a short-term Sunday school class on the subject at church."

"Oh! That would be good! I'll have to talk it over with Pastor when we get home and see what he thinks about it. What about you? Where do you see yourself in a few years with the police department?" Taysia pushed the last quarter of her food aside, too full to finish it.

He traced the grain in the tabletop with one

finger. "I'm not sure, exactly. I've actually toyed with going private. Maybe becoming a PI."

"Really? What would make you want to do that?"

He shrugged. "More money. But there is more financial risk, too. You have to obtain all your own equipment. Then there's insurance. And the income isn't steady, so there would be a lot of adjustment to going that route. I'm still praying about it."

They talked about their hopes and dreams all the way to the zoo thirty minutes away. And by the time they arrived, Taysia knew she was hopelessly, head over heels in love with Kylen Sumner once more.

Kylen had never felt more miserable than he did as he pulled his car into the parking lot at the zoo's southern gate.

He loved the woman at his side with all his heart. He loved her wit and charm. Loved that she had overcome the hard things in her life and molded them to help others. Loved her heart that longed to prevent other women from living with some of the hurts she'd experienced. Loved that she loved his God.

And the thought that he might never have a future with her was killing him little by little on the inside. He hadn't meant to rush her last night.

He'd known it was too soon to tell her he loved her the minute the words had slipped past his lips. But there was no taking them back. And it was the truth. There was no other woman for him. He just hoped God wasn't going to ask him to live single for the rest of his life. Because he was enjoying her company too much to want to give it up. What was he going to do if she never could fall in love with him?

As he slipped the money into the correct slot on the parking payment box, he shook off the melancholy. He would worry about that if the time came to worry about it. For now, he was going to enjoy her company and have a blast of a day.

He paid for their tickets and glanced at her as they entered the zoo. "Where to first?"

She looked around, then took the map from him. "I don't know. How about there?" She pointed to an African village straight ahead.

"Oooh, Africa." He smirked and jostled her arm. "There's a large animal that is very prominent there, you know."

"I know." A small smile quirked the corner of her mouth, and her eyes opened wide with feigned innocence. "Rhinos *are* pretty large, and it would be cool to see one, but I don't see them on the map."

He laughed and took her hand. "Africa it is. And we might even see some—"

"Don't say it!" She gave him a friendly punch.

"What's wrong with giraffes? I was going to say giraffes."

She angled him a look. "Uh-huh."

He grinned shamelessly and pulled her into the viewing area made to look like a village schoolhouse.

Zebras grazed placidly in a meadow, with giraffes munching on food from high feeding troughs just behind them.

Taysia stepped close to his side and leaned her head against his shoulder. "They're beautiful. It would be so neat to see them in the wild one day."

He glanced down at her. "An African safari? You'd like to go on one, huh?"

"Yes, I would love to. Our church is going out to help build an orphanage next summer. I've been toying with whether or not to go. I just don't know how I would handle Mom's Gym."

They ambled farther along the path and stepped into an aviary. Kylen draped his arm around her shoulders as they studied the colorful African birds.

"The mission trip is two weeks long, and then I figured while I was over there I might as well take some time and have a little vacation. So I'd be gone for at least three weeks; I just don't know if I can leave the gym on its own for that long."

Weaverbirds built nests that hung down from tree branches like large brown Christmas balls. He admired one little yellow bird hanging upside down and busily working a stem of grass like a tiny seamstress. "What about leaving Marie in charge?"

Taysia cringed. "That would never work."

"Why not? She did great with that crying pregnant lady the other day. You said so yourself."

"Yeah. She did do fine with her. I was kinda surprised." She dropped her head guiltily and pretended to be studying a small bird under a bush.

Kylen bit back a smile. She loved that girl like a little sister, he could tell. Squeezing her shoulders, he said, "She's had a great teacher and example to learn from."

She glanced up at him. "Thanks, Ky. That was a nice thing to say."

He tapped her nose. "It was a true thing to say."

"Well"—she spread her hands—"it is a moot point because she would never be able to teach the classes. She doesn't have the training."

"You have a whole year," he reminded. "And the classes she's not qualified to teach, when the time comes, you could hire a temporary instructor to fill." He hoped she would do this. It would be good for her to get away for a few weeks.

Taysia cocked her head. "That might work."

"See?" He grinned as he opened the exit door of the aviary and held it for her. "You're in the company of a genius!"

She smiled and gave him a peck on the cheek as she went by. "I just might be."

The rest of the day passed by too quickly for Kylen's liking. At noon they watched a birds of prey show with gorgeous falcons, eagles, and ospreys swooping and diving to signals from their trainers. Of course he had to give Taysia a little ribbing when they stopped at the elephant viewing area, about how placid and unscary the lumbering beasts looked. And now the day was winding down, and they were almost back to the gate they'd started out at that morning. Taysia folded her arms along the top rail of the fence of the flamingo exhibit and rested her chin on her wrist as she studied the birds.

Kylen stuffed his hands into his pockets and admitted to himself that he was doing more studying of the beautiful woman beside him than he was of the zoo animals.

She sighed. "They aren't as pink as I imagined they would be."

He tore his focus from her and looked at one of the gangly, backward-legged birds. "Looks more...orange than pink."

"Coral."

"Right. Coral."

"Still, they're beautiful."

He brushed a strand of hair back from her face. "Lots of beauty around here."

Her face flushed to rival the insides of a

watermelon, and Kylen felt his chest tighten. He let his fingers linger and toyed with the golden strand of her hair. She looked at him then, and there was such a look of longing in her eyes, he felt it like a bullet to a flak jacket. All the air left his lungs.

"I can do this, Kylen. With God's help, I'm going to get past all our crashing waves and move on. I realized last night that it was my pride keeping me from letting go of the past. Love is somewhat about making yourself vulnerable to the other person. And I've been keeping you at arm's length"—she cringed—"well, *trying* to keep you at arm's length, as sort of a self-preservation—to protect myself from getting hurt again. I don't want to do that anymore." She stood to her full height and stepped closer to him.

Kylen could hardly breathe for the rapid beating of his heart in his throat. He swallowed.

"Ky, I love you, too. I'm sorry I couldn't—"

He laid his thumb across her lips to stop her apology. "It's okay, Layne. We're here now. That's all that matters." He kissed her then, not caring that they were standing in the middle of the observation area in full view of everyone around them. And from her response, he was glad they were in a very public area, because she hadn't kissed him like she was kissing him now in a very long time.

"EWWW! That's GROSS!" A little boy stopped beside them.

Taysia smiled against his lips, and they turned their heads as one to look down at the little guy.

A mop of dark, curly hair spilled in unruly abandon over the top of his head, and glittering brown eyes studied them with undisguised curiosity.

"Sammy! Leave them alone!" The tyke's mortified mother snatched his arm and dragged him farther down the path, leaving them relatively alone once again.

Kylen leaned his forehead against hers. "I love you."

She pressed a quick kiss to his lips. "I love you, too."

Contentment bubbled over on a sigh, and he stepped back, snagging her hand as he did so. "Come on, we still have the spider-slash-creepy-crawly exhibit to go see." He pumped his eyebrows and tossed her a wink.

She rolled her eyes. "Oh, yeah, *that* ought to be fun."

Her phone rang as they started down the path.

Taysia fumbled in her purse for her phone. She couldn't remember the last time she'd felt this content. She was so glad she'd finally gotten up the courage to admit her feelings to Kylen. God was good, and they were going to make it past this.

The number wasn't one she recognized. She debated over whether to answer it as it rang for the third time, then decided just to take it. Pressing the answer button, she lifted the phone to her ear. "Hello?"

"Hi, Taysia, this is Loraine."

Loraine...Loraine...? Loraine *who*?

"I met you the other night. I was with your father..."

"Oh! Yes, of course. Hi, Loraine. What can I do for you?"

"Well, honey, I'm afraid I have some bad news."

Taysia's heart lurched, and she jerked to a halt right in the middle of the path. "What happened?"

Kylen turned to study her with a worried frown.

Loraine was still talking. "First, I want you to know your daddy is fine. But he's in the hospital."

Taysia pulled free of Kylen and pressed her hand to her forehead. "Hospital?" The question sounded dim-witted even to her own ears, but nothing else would come to mind.

"Yes, dear. He's had a mini stroke. They are going to keep him overnight for observation, but think he should be able to go home in the morning."

"A stroke...how bad? Does he have paralysis?"

"No, honey. He seems to have full feeling. The doctors are calling it a mini stroke and will do some more follow-up tests today and tomorrow. We'll know more after a while."

"Oh, good. Okay. Well...I'm up in Seattle, but"—she glanced at Kylen, and he was already nodding and prompting her to follow him to the exit—"we're leaving right now. I'll get there just as soon as I can. Thank you for calling me."

"Of course, honey. I would have called you sooner, but your daddy couldn't remember your number, and his phone was in his pants, and they confiscated those in the ER the minute we got here and didn't bring them back until just now." She giggled like a schoolgirl. "Can't say that I mind, though. Ever since I found out he was going to be fine, I haven't been able to stop staring at his legs in that sexy hospital gown he's wearing."

"Oh, pshaw!" Daddy's voice filtered through the line, and Taysia could tell Loraine was doing her part to keep him in good spirits. Maybe she was all right, this woman her daddy was dating.

She smiled as Kylen led her through the turnstile exit. "I'm glad you're there with him, Loraine. Don't let him give any of the nurses a bad time."

"I won't, honey. And I've got your number in my phone now, so if anything else happens before you get here, I'll be sure to call right away. You drive careful now. I'll wager you're with a certain new police officer from the Marinville force?"

"Yes...how did you know?"

"Oh, word travels fast in a town like this, child. My neighbor, Mrs. Conoughy, saw you two driving out of town together yesterday."

"Oh." Kylen held the car door for her, and she sank into her seat. "Well, we're on our way. Give Daddy my love, and I'll see you around..." She checked her watch. "Seven thirty."

"Okay, I'll tell him."

She hung up and told Kylen what had happened.

He squeezed her hand as they pulled out of the parking lot and headed for the freeway. "Let's pray for him right quick." Kylen prayed quietly as he drove, and Taysia leaned her head back and closed her eyes. As she listened to him pray for her daddy, she knew she had found the man she wanted to spend the rest of her life with.

Chapter 10

Loraine and Daddy were watching the first round of *Jeopardy* when Taysia and Kylen arrived at the hospital room.

Loraine lowered the volume on the TV.

Daddy stretched out a gnarled hand and smiled. “Hey, Snookums!”

The tension in Taysia’s shoulders eased, and tears filled her eyes and fell across her cheeks. She hadn’t realized how worried she’d been until this moment. “Daddy, I’m so glad you are alright!” She bent over his bed and pulled him into a firm hug.

“Bah!” He patted her back and then grasped her shoulders and put her from him. “It wasn’t anything. You know doctors. Always needing someone new to poke and prod.”

Taysia glanced over at Loraine.

Lips pinched together in a firm, straight line and eyes narrowed, she leaned forward and slapped Daddy on the leg. “Don’t you make light of this, Dale Green! She’s your daughter, and she deserves to know what is going on in your life!"

Daddy cleared his throat and toyed with the edge of his blanket.

Kylen reached out and touched Taysia's shoulder. "I'm going to go down to the cafeteria and get us something to eat before they close...Snookums."

Taysia stilled and tossed him a friendly glare. "Now see what you've done, Daddy?"

The patient chuckled and glanced back and forth between them, a speculative gleam in his eye.

With a light smile and a tug on her hair, Kylen said, "I'll bring you up something in a few minutes."

"Thanks." She gave his arm a swat as he left her side.

Thankful for the moment of privacy Kylen had just granted them and the lightness he'd injected into the room, she turned back to Daddy. "Tell me everything that happened, Daddy. Please?"

Daddy peeked at Loraine, who folded her arms and lowered her chin with the air of a woman ready to do battle.

Taysia suppressed a grin. She liked this woman more and more each time she met her.

Waving a hand as though shooing away a pesky fly, Daddy turned back to her. "Really, it wasn't anything serious. You don't need to worry about me."

Loraine cleared her throat.

Daddy rolled his eyes and continued, "I woke up this morning feeling a little funny. Loraine was supposed to come over, and we were going to go golfing. By the time she got to the house, I couldn't seem to put two thoughts together. She called 9-1-1, and the paramedics brought me here. I don't remember much in between waking up and seeing the doctor here."

Loraine dropped the battle-ax air, and Taysia could see tears glimmering in her eyes. "I was never so scared in all my born days! I asked him which of our cars he wanted to take, and he couldn't even form an answer. His words were all slurred, and he almost fell when he let go of the door to reach for his coat." She brushed her fingers under each eye. "I got him to the couch and called for help. Thankfully by the time we got here, he was back to his normal, cranky self."

Taysia pulled the woman into a tight hug.

Loraine's body tensed, momentarily startled by the abrupt embrace.

Taysia didn't let go. "I'm so thankful you were there to help him. Thank you!"

The tension eased from Loraine's shoulders. And her arms tightened around Taysia. "Me too, dolly. Me too."

Pulling back, Taysia moved to stand by Daddy's side. "So the doctors say you are going to be all right?"

"Yes. They want me to take some blood thinners. But they say I should pretty much be back to normal in a couple days."

"Thank the Lord!"

Kylen returned a few moments later with a tray of food, and they chatted for a few more minutes. But soon Taysia could see Daddy flagging and trying not to show it.

She stood. "We should be going, Daddy, so you can get some sleep. What time are you getting out tomorrow?"

"Should be in the morning sometime, but Loraine will be here to help me get home."

Loraine nodded assurance to that statement.

"Okay. Well, I'll come by and check on you before church tomorrow, okay?"

Daddy waved a hand. "No need for you to rush around so early. After church is fine. And Taysia?"

"Yes?"

"Say a prayer for your old man at church tomorrow, would you?"

Taysia blinked away tears. "You bet I will, Daddy."

Kylen stretched out his hand. "Glad you are going to be fine, Mr. Green. I'll be praying for you, as well."

"Thank you, son. And it's Dale."

Out at the elevators, as Kylen pushed the button, Taysia arched a brow at him. "That was a high compliment coming from Daddy."

"What?"

"Him telling you to call him Dale."

"Really?"

"Mmm-hmm." The elevator doors slid open and they stepped inside. "Not even Blaine has been given that privilege, and I've been seeing him off and on for over a year."

"Well"—he shrugged—"Blaine's not as good for you as I am." His lips spread in a wide grin.

Taysia chuckled. "And not since Moses has such a humble man as yourself walked the face of the earth?"

"Well, Jesus was here between Moses and me, so I wouldn't go that far."

She laughed again.

"No." His face turned suddenly serious, and he reached for her hand. "I didn't mean that I was better than Blaine. Just better for *you*."

Warmth traced her spine, and she leaned up on her toes to give him a quick kiss. "You're right."

She started to pull away, but he leaned after her and captured her mouth with his again. After only a moment, he framed her face with his hands and rested his forehead against hers.

"I had a great time this weekend. Thanks for coming with me."

She wanted to kiss him again, but the way her knees had turned to jelly, she knew she didn't dare. "I had fun too. Sorry Daddy kinda cut our day short."

The elevator doors slid open, and they stepped out into the hospital's garage.

Kylen tugged her in the direction of the

Mustang, his fingers laced between hers. "So. Tomorrow we meet with Sophia, don't forget."

Taysia sighed. "How could I forget?"

He gave her hand a squeeze. "It's going to be fine. I think she is ready to drop the lawsuit, if you give her a free year's membership to the gym."

Fisherman's Wharf pulsed with the bustle of waiters rushing to satisfy clientele, the clang of patrons' utensils on plates, and the clash of clumsy busboys clearing tables. Kylen was glad for the noisy crowd. It meant that even though he was alone at a table with Sophia, he wasn't really alone with her. He looked around the room; at a waiter hurrying by; at a child across the way tossing spaghetti on the floor while his parents argued with quiet heat; out the window where a white sail poked a hole in the azure blue of the oceanic slate; anywhere but at Sophia, who hadn't taken her calculating eyes off him since he showed up.

Under the table he rubbed his hands together. Somehow, whenever he was in her presence, he couldn't help but feel like a skittish gazelle locked in a cage with a hungry lioness.

Today her clothes only added to his discomfort. The neckline of her scant, filmy black top plunged embarrassingly low. The thing was more like a pair of wide suspenders than a shirt. Kylen shifted in his chair and eyed the entry, wishing Taysia would hurry up.

"So…" Sophia hunched over the table and toyed with the straw in her moisture-frosted glass with a long red fingernail. "Are you busy later? After we're done talking things over with Taysia?"

Kylen met her eyes and felt the first twinge of sympathy for her. What must it be like to be so unsure of yourself that you had to try and seduce your way into a relationship? She hadn't been like this in high school. Catty, yes. Haughty, yes. But loose and easy had never been her style. She'd started down this path when Jim dumped her for the first time.

"Why do you do this to yourself?"

She pulled back. "What?"

A gesture took in her attire. "This."

She smirked and took a sultry sip of her drink. "So you did notice…you don't like my outfit?"

Kylen swallowed and took a different tack. "Where'd you meet the last guy you dated?"

Sophia shrugged. "Down at Pete's."

The local bar. Of course. "And how did that work out for you?"

"Jed was a deadbeat. He didn't like Jimmy." She quirked a penciled brow.

Kylen softened at the mention of her son. "Where's Jimmy now? I'd like to meet him sometime."

Her whole face transformed, and she actually

smiled without trying to be seductive. "He's at my mom's. She watches him for me whenever I need her to, and he loves going to Grammy's." She looked out the window and studied the ocean horizon, finally adding, "He's a good kid; I think you would like him."

"I'm sure I would." Kylen drew a pattern in the water droplets on his glass. "Don't you want to give Jimmy a better life than what the next idiot from Pete's has to offer?"

Her head snapped toward him, and fire blazed in her eyes. "Don't you judge me, Kylen Sumner. Mr. 'I have my life all together.' Besides"—she leaned forward, easily transforming into the seductress once more—"I'm here with you. And I know you wouldn't be anything like Jed."

Gesturing for her to stop, Kylen met her gaze. "That's not what I was doing. Trust me, Sophia, if anybody needed to get his life together, it was me. With God's help I'm working my way toward that. But I simply meant that the way you are dressing, for starters, is going to attract a certain type of guy. Guys like—Jed."

She huffed and studied the ocean once more. "Yes. Jed." Her voice was flat. Lifeless. "Sometimes you have to take companionship where you can find it, Kylen."

"You were meant for more than that, Sophia."

She chuckled and angled her eyes toward him. "So now you are going to try and save my soul?"

Kylen sighed. "Would that I could. Only you

can make the choice to do that, Sophia."

She waved a hand. "Yeah, yeah. I remember the Sunday school lessons."

Kylen pressed his lips together, holding his silence. He remembered, now, that Sophia's parents had been churchgoing people back in high school. Sophia had often mocked her parents' beliefs with him and their friends. If only he hadn't joined her in that. Now, his life would have to speak for him. He didn't know what to say that would change her mind about the way she was living. But he had to try. "They aren't just stories, Soph. They are lessons. Ones that can change your life for the better if you'll heed them."

She smirked. "Well, Kylen, you've always been too perfect for your own good."

"You and I both know that's a lie."

Something behind him caught her attention. Her lips thinned into a sultry smile, and she met his gaze once more. "Maybe the bad boy in you is what makes me like you so much."

Kylen made a dismissive gesture of protest.

Abruptly, she stood and said, "I'll be right back." She started past him, her eyes fixed on some point near the entry.

Kylen was just turning to see what had caught her attention when the ankle on one of her ridiculously high heels twisted, and she sprawled into his lap. Before he knew what was happening, Sophia Clinesmith had both arms around his neck, and had planted her lips firmly against his own.

Taysia pulled into the parking space next to Kylen's convertible and rested her forehead against the steering wheel.

Thankfulness that Daddy was going to be fine washed over her. After church, she'd run by the hospital and chatted with him and Loraine. Daddy would be released within the hour. He was just waiting for the doctor to come by on his rounds to sign him out. He'd looked better today, his color was up, and more of his usual spunk glittered in his eyes. Loraine had promised to drive him home and sit with him until Taysia could get to his place later today. Taysia planned to sleep on Daddy's couch for a couple days to make sure he was really 100 percent on the mend before he was left on his own again.

Climbing out of the car, she smiled. Maybe Kylen would come with her this evening. She played a mean game of chess and would like the opportunity to beat him a couple times. Daddy's board was always set up and waiting by the fireplace.

The sight of the beautiful Fisherman's Wharf reminded her of the need to switch gears and get her mind on working out this situation with Sophia. Her heels clicked rapidly across the fitted stones. A glance out across the bay filled her with awe as she hurried up the walk toward the restaurant entrance. Today the ocean seemed to be smooth as glass. A single cloud, cottony white, floated in the distance, looking forlorn against the blue backdrop of the sky. The darkened glass walls of the Fisherman's Wharf reflected the bay with mirrorlike perfection.

With a sigh and a mumbled prayer for patience with Sophia, Taysia pulled open one of the large doors and hurried inside. The foyer was glassed in but wide open to the whole restaurant. The builders of this place had wanted patrons to have an unobstructed view of the ocean no matter where they were standing. A quick perusal of the tables to her right didn't reveal Kylen and Sophia. But Blaine was there, having lunch with his parents. *Great.* She smiled and gave a little wave when he looked up and saw her. He nodded his head toward a table at the other end of the restaurant, but as he glanced past her, his eyes rounded.

Taysia spun back to her left and froze.

She blinked. Forgot to breathe. Blinked again. *Oh Lord, no. Please. I'm not seeing that.*

But she was indeed seeing Sophia, in a skimpy black outfit, sitting on Kylen's lap. And kissing him.

With a huff that came out more as a roar, Taysia did an about-face and stormed back to her car. Familiar hurt and anger and pain rushed in on a tidal wave that nearly blinded her.

With a startled grunt, Kylen pushed Sophia away and held her firmly at arm's length. At the same time, he heard a sound from the entryway that made his blood run cold. He turned to see Taysia, just disappearing out the door. She'd obviously seen—what? How much had she seen?

"Sophia!" He gave her a little shake, his anger surging so close to the surface that he feared to say more. Well aware of what he might do if he kept his hands on her for even another second, he jerked away from her.

With a startled gasp, she stumbled back. The three-inch spike on her black shoe caught against the carpet, and she sprawled over backward, landing in an ungainly heap on the floor. Gasps from several people filled the room.

Kylen stood. Looked down at her, then out the window to where he could see the parking lot. Taysia's little blue car was just backing out of the space next to his Mustang. Reaching down, he yanked her to her feet, and none too gently. "This might be the lowest thing you've ever done, Sophia."

He dug in his wallet and tossed a five-dollar bill down to cover his drink, then rushed out the door, leaving Sophia behind to pay her own way without so much as a goodbye.

Taysia's key fob took three presses before it finally popped the lock. Yanking open the door, she glared at Kylen's shiny red Mustang. She could think of better things to do with her keys right about now. Instead she dropped into her seat, cranked the key so hard that the starter made a scary grinding noise, and then peeled out of the lot. She turned right onto the narrow coastal highway and laid the pedal to the floor. The landscape blurred as it whizzed by. A car blared its horn as she squealed around a corner in the wrong lane. She had the presence of mind to slow down a little then, but the scene from the restaurant kept flashing over and over in her mind.

Oh, Lord. Oh, Lord. Oh, Lord. It was the only prayer she could come up with.

The tears didn't come until she pulled into the park overlooking Mossy Rock Point, and then they came by the bucketful. She didn't have any tissues, but she found an old workout shirt on the floor in the backseat and sobbed into it until it was damp and limp.

Tossing the shirt aside, she slammed her palm against the steering wheel. It felt so good that she hit it again. And again. *I'm such a fool!*

Tipping her head back against the seat, she stared at a spot on the ceiling and smeared at her cheeks with the flats of her fingers. *God, why did You let this happen to me again?*

Silence bounced off the windows and upholstery.

Seizing a forgotten scrunchie, she shoved open her door, scraped her hair back from her face, and strode down the path toward the sand. When she reached the shore, she kicked off her shoes and waded out into ankle-deep water.

Her heart felt vacant. Used. Like all the times in elementary school when she'd known she was the butt of a joke, but pretended to laugh along with the other kids.

Wrapping her arms around herself, she looked up toward the sky and closed her eyes, letting the sun dry her tears.

You can do this. You'll just go back to the way things were and keep putting one foot in front of the other.

A grimace twisted her lips. What a lame little pep talk. Oh, how she hated that he'd fooled her, again!

"Kylen Sumner, I HATE YOU!" she screamed across the waves.

"Do you?"

She spun around, spraying droplets of water in every direction, her heart hammering in her ears.

Kylen stood there, hands resting casually in the pockets of his slacks. And, blast the man, his eyes were shiny, like he was trying to hold tears at bay.

Taysia gave a dismissive sniff and turned her back on him. "Go away. I do not want to talk to you right now."

"I know what you saw looked bad, Layne, but—"

Spinning, she kicked a stream of water at him. "I said, 'Go AWAY!'" She was acting like a two-year-old. She needed to get a grip. Her shoulders slumped. "Just go."

Instead of leaving, he stepped toward her. "Layne..." He stretched out one hand. "Just hear me out..."

Her eyes narrowed. "I'm done hearing you out, Kylen! Done!" She pushed past him and snatched up her sandals. Skirt balled into one fist, she stomped up the trail toward her car. Halfway up, she couldn't resist a glance down toward the beach. His back to her, Kylen stood still, head hanging down. A wave washed in farther than the others and sloshed over his dress shoes, but he didn't move. A small twinge snagged her heartbeat, but she kept going. Good. Let him be the one to feel a little pain for a change!

Daddy moved his queen one space and proudly proclaimed, "Checkmate!"

"Oh, I didn't even see that move." Taysia knocked her king over and did her best to offer a smile and look perky.

Leaning back in his chair, Daddy tilted his head and studied her for a long moment. "You're not yourself this evening."

Taysia picked up their teacups. "I'm fine, Daddy. Can I get you some more tea?"

Daddy pursed his lips and pierced her with another look.

She blinked innocently.

He sighed. "Sure. Why don't you bring it in by the couch?"

Taysia made her escape, thankful for the moment of reprieve from Daddy's perceptive scrutiny.

She took her time in the kitchen. Put the cookies she'd baked earlier into Daddy's cookie jar. Wiped down the counters. Loaded the last of the dishes into the dishwasher. Dipped, dipped, dipped the tea bags into the hot water in the cups. All of it mechanically. All while replaying the stupid, horrible revelation from the restaurant and rethinking every nuance of Kylen's face when he'd caught up with her on the beach.

Daddy appeared in the entry and leaned his shoulder into the wall.

"Sorry I'm taking so long. I wanted to do a little cleaning up while I was in here. The tea is almost ready."

Hands clasped loosely, he studied her, chin tilted down and head canted to one side. His silence and the understanding in his wise eyes were almost her undoing.

Taysia swallowed and wrapped the string of the tea bag around the spoon to squeeze the last drops into the cup. The cupboard door creaked when she opened it to toss the spent leaves into the garbage can. Without meeting Daddy's gaze, she turned and reached for the sugar bowl.

Daddy sighed. "So. He's broken your heart again."

The teaspoon chattered against the rim, and Taysia gritted her teeth, willing away the trembling in her hands. She was here to be strong for Daddy tonight. He needed to rest, not worry about her.

Suddenly he was there beside her. "Ah, darling, come here." He set aside the sugar and turned her into his embrace.

And that bit of gentleness was more than her composure could bear. The sobs started deep under her rib cage and shook her whole body as she buried her face in her hands and collapsed into the comfort of Daddy's warm arms. Even though age had shortened his stature, her head still fit under his chin, and she relaxed into his strength and settled in.

"There now." The stroke of his hand along the length of her hair and the kiss he pressed to her forehead were more comfort than any words of consolation he could ever offer. And he simply held her.

For how long, she didn't know. But when she stepped back, there were wet tear streaks marring the front of his shirt, and she brushed at them with her fingers. "Sorry."

Tucking a length of her hair behind her ear, Daddy cupped her cheek against his palm and looked deep into her eyes. "Tell me what happened, honey."

She stared at the wet tracks. "I saw him"—her lips trembled—"k-kissing Sophia."

"Clinesmith!?"

She nodded.

Sighing, Daddy leaned back into the counter and folded his arms. "Tell me everything. Start at the beginning."

So Taysia laid it all out for him. How they'd been supposed to meet at Fisherman's Wharf to discuss the lawsuit. How Kylen thought he'd talked Sophia into settling. How she'd found them when she walked in the door. And how she'd lit out of there and Kylen had followed her to the beach.

"Wait a minute! One minute he's in the restaurant kissing Sophia, and then he followed you to the beach? What did he say?"

"He said he knew that what I'd seen looked bad but he wanted to explain. I told him I was done giving him any more chances and left him standing there."

Daddy's eyebrows disappeared under his thatch of silver hair. "You didn't give him the chance to tell his side of the story?"

Taysia gripped her head and then raised her

hands in the air. "What is there for him to explain? I saw what he was doing with my own two eyes!"

Daddy shrugged. "The man just didn't seem like the type to be a two-timer, that's all. I think you should at least give him a chance to tell his side of the story."

She couldn't believe what she was hearing. "You're taking his side?"

"I'm not taking his side, just pointing out that you should probably at least hear him out."

"I'm going to bed. Call me if you need anything in the night." Taysia stalked out of the kitchen and plopped down on the couch where earlier she'd laid out bedding. Fluffing the pillow and curling her arm under it, she closed her eyes with every intention of dropping right off to sleep.

But the memory of Kylen's eyes when he'd found her on the beach haunted her. Why would he follow her, if he'd moved on and was with Sophia now? And why would he have had tears in his eyes? Her own eyes flooded again, her broken heart spilling over and flowing down into her hair.

She'd forgotten the aching torment that came along with shattered expectations. Lord help her, she didn't know if she could go on breathing. Pressing the heels of her hands into her eyes, as though pressure could stop the flood, she heaved in a shuddering breath. Then another. And another. She could do this. She had to do this. There were no other choices.

Sleep was fitful, but she awoke with the determination to put this behind her and get on with her life.

Today she had to teach two classes, then she would go talk things over with Blaine.

Chapter 11

Later in the afternoon, Taysia pulled into the parking lot at Blaine's apartment complex and eased into one of the tiny spots made available for visitors. The old green pickup that Blaine had driven ever since she could remember sat in his assigned space. She sighed and fiddled with her car keys, glancing out the glass toward his door. If she did this, there would be no going back. She sniffed. Who was she kidding? She had nothing to go *back* to.

Slowly she climbed out and took the steps up to his door.

He answered it in his stocking feet, but still wearing his slacks and dress shirt from his day of teaching at the high school. His tie hung loose, the knot resting halfway down his chest. Eyes widening, his brows arched. "Hi." He stepped back and gestured her inside.

Clink, clink, clink. Her car keys, twirling around one finger, smacked against the palm of her hand, and she seemed to be frozen to the spot, unable to move. "You sure?" Tears pricked the backs of her eyes.

"Come on in, Taysia." He sighed. "I knew you would come; I just didn't expect you this soon."

In the living room, he quickly moved a spread of books from the couch. He'd obviously been studying.

"I'm interrupting. I should go."

"No. You're fine. Please sit. We need to talk." He set the stack of books on the coffee table and waited for her to take a seat. "Can I get you a soda? Coffee? Tea?"

"No. Thanks, I'm fine." The irony of that phrase struck her then. How easily the lie slipped off her tongue. She stuffed her keys into her purse and set it on the floor.

Easing his hands into his pockets, Blaine stayed on his feet. He kicked at a mark on his tan carpet and kept his silence.

"Blaine, I...I don't know what to say. You were right. I never should have trusted him. But"—she paused, trying to come up with the easiest way to say this—"I needed to come by and tell you that it won't work between you and me. I'd love to be friends, but..."

His face paled, and then he flinched as the words hit him full force. "So I'm second best, and even then not good enough, huh?" He looked away, not meeting her gaze.

She felt awful. "Blaine, you are good enough.

Just, you and I, we could never...I could never...not now. And it wouldn't be fair to you for me to pretend otherwise."

He huffed a quick bark of laughter. "I know. I knew the minute I heard he was back in town that it was the end for you and me. But I hoped I was wrong. You two always had that certain spark when you were together."

"I'm not going to be with Kylen, Blaine. He ensured that. But I realized over these past couple weeks that what I feel for you is simply friendship and nothing stronger."

Lips pinched together, he studied his toe as it made patterns in the carpet. "I think you're probably right."

Standing, Taysia dug for her keys. "I'm glad you understand, Blaine. I just...well...you said when he broke my heart you would be waiting. But I just can't do a relationship right now."

He opened his mouth and started to say something, then snapped it shut again.

"What?"

He pierced her with a look, then turned back to his carpet art. "I think Sophia set up that little scene at the restaurant."

Taysia took a step back as all the blood in her body swirled down toward her toes. "What do you mean?"

"I mean, for fifteen minutes before you got there, she and Kylen talked sporadically, but Kylen looked pretty uncomfortable to be there alone with her. He kept turning around and looking at the entry like he was waiting for someone. Obviously you. Then the next thing I knew, you walked in the door, and as I nodded you in the direction of their table, Sophia's ankle twisted and she landed in Kylen's lap and laid that kiss on him. You took off so fast you didn't see it, but Kylen practically shoved her over in his hurry to push her away. She actually fell onto the floor, and for a second I thought he would leave her lying there. But he helped her up, said something to her, and then took off out the door." He grimaced. "I tried to call you last night to tell you, but you weren't answering at home or on your cell."

"I stayed at Daddy's. And I turned my phone off." Taysia heard her voice as though it were coming from a million miles away.

Blaine stepped toward her, took her elbow, and eased her back down onto his couch. "Listen, you and Kylen, much as I hate to admit it, well, you two have something special. I wanted that for us, but I knew that first day at church. You never looked at me the way you looked at him. Just don't throw away a good thing because of a jealous biddy like Sophia."

The words she'd snapped at Kylen on the beach the day before traipsed across her memory, and Taysia placed her palm to her forehead. "Oh, Blaine, it may already be too late."

The drive across town to Kylen's house was the longest drive she'd ever taken. Each block stretched on interminably, and every car in town seemed to pull out in front of her. All of them puttered along, simply out to enjoy the spring tulips that were beginning to pop up in all the window boxes. It was all Taysia could do to keep from laying on the horn as Mr. Sinclair sat at the stop sign trying to decide if he wanted to turn right and no doubt head to Pete's Bar, or left and probably visit his old friend Charlie. After he had looked both ways at least a dozen times, his old gray Ford LTD began the left-hand turn. But he stopped suddenly. Taysia squawked and slammed on the brakes. Waving apologetically in the rearview mirror, Mr. Sinclair swung a wide turn to the right. Taysia rolled her eyes. Apparently Pete's booze held more appeal than Charlie's company.

Finally she pulled into Kylen's drive and sat staring at his door. She couldn't see his car, but mostly he parked it in the third bay of the garage unless he was just dropping by home for a moment.

Her legs had all the strength of cooked spaghetti as she stepped onto the drive. Leaning on her door for a moment, she took a big breath, then started up the steps as she prayed he'd be able to find it in himself to forgive her. She hesitated only a moment before knocking. Holding her breath, she studied the porch rail to her left as she waited. After a long lull, she released the breath in a puff, pulled in another long draw of air, and knocked again. Still no reply.

Taysia descended the steps of his porch and headed around the corner, where she stood on tiptoe and peered into the garage door windows, hands cupped by her eyes. Both Kylen's squad car and his convertible were inside.

She sighed and glanced at her watch. So he was inside ignoring her, or he had gone for a jog. Either way she was going to miss him. She'd promised Daddy she'd have dinner ready at five thirty, and he'd already invited Loraine over.

Hurrying to her car, she snatched up a clean napkin from the floor between her seats. Snagging a pen from her purse, she wrote, "Kylen, I'm sorry I doubted you. Please call me. I'll be at Daddy's." Even though she knew he had her number, she scrawled it at the bottom. She signed it simply "Layne," then hurried up the steps and tucked the note into Kylen's mailbox, where she could still see today's mail. When he got home and picked up the mail, he'd find it.

She'd wanted to talk to him in person, but they would just have to talk on the phone later.

Right now, she needed to get to the grocery store for some last-minute purchases before dinner.

Taysia sliced onions and green peppers and sautéed them in butter, then set them aside and eyed her silent phone. With a sigh she scooped the long slices of steak into the pan and seared them, then seasoned them with a dash of garlic, onion powder, salt, and pepper.

Still the phone pulsed silence.

Scooping a can of refried beans into a saucepan, Taysia turned the heat on low and set to grating cheese and chopping lettuce, tomatoes, and avocados.

Fajitas were one of Daddy's favorite meals.

The doorbell rang, and she heard the rustle of Daddy's paper as he called, "I'll get it!" A moment later he greeted Loraine.

Taysia released a breath she hadn't even noticed she'd been holding.

This is all your own fault. If you had just trusted him and stayed around to see what was going on, you would have seen the truth.

Admitting her culpability didn't make her feel any better.

Sprinkling the fajita seasoning on the meat, she added a little water and gave it a stir.

"Mmmmmm! Smells great in here!" Loraine scooted up behind her and gave her a squeeze.

Taysia smiled. "Hi, Loraine." She turned and gave the woman a full embrace.

After a moment Loraine put her out at arm's length and studied her intently. "So what's the matter?"

With a dismissive smile and wave of her hand, she faced the stove. "Oh, I'm fine. How was your day?"

"Now none of that, missy! I can tell that something is amiss. And Dale told me about your conversation last night. So, come on, I want to hear the whole story from you, yourself."

Realizing the woman was as tenacious as a dog on a scent, Taysia gave in. She confessed the whole sorry mess as she turned off the heat, added the peppers and onions to the pot, and then scooped the whole concoction into a serving bowl. Between trips to the table, she told about her conversation with Blaine and how she'd gone to Kylen's house and ended up leaving him a note.

With a satisfied nod, Loraine took her seat at the table and proclaimed in a perky voice, "Well then, I suspect we'll be hearing from the young man before the night is through. Let's eat."

Daddy grinned and tossed Taysia a wink.

And for the first time that day, Taysia felt herself ease into a genuine smile.

Loraine was probably right. Kylen would at least come talk to her when he saw the note. He would probably be knocking on the door any minute.

It was late when Kylen got home from the long jog he'd decided to take this afternoon. He hadn't slept at all the night before, and he'd wanted to drain himself today so he'd at least be able to sleep tonight. He'd run along the coastal highway until he knew he had to turn back or never make the run home.

He jogged all the way to his porch steps and then collapsed onto the top one and lay back onto the deck. His heart was pounding so hard he could feel it knocking against his breastbone, and sweat dripped from every surface of his body. The weariness felt good. Numbing. He heaved great gulps of air, then forced himself to stand and walk around the yard. As he cooled down, hands on his hips, he studied the sprinkling of stars that glittered in the night sky. He pulled a long stream of air in through his nose and pushed it out through pursed lips. So distant, they looked so cold. Another inhale and exhale. Yet the ice-chip stars were really burning orbs of gas. He snorted. Appearances could be so deceiving.

He glanced toward Taysia's house. Her car wasn't in the drive. She was probably staying away out of fear he might come over and confront her. What a mess. Pain squeezed his heart. She had to be feeling so betrayed right now. But no more than he was by the fact that she still trusted him so little. He wasn't ready to give up on her, but right now she needed a little time. He sighed. Would they ever get beyond the waves of doubt and distrust?

The exhaustion hit him after only a few more moments, and he pushed through his door and only paused for a quick rinse in the shower before he fell into bed. He was asleep almost before his head hit the pillow.

The call came first thing in the morning. Kylen groaned and let it ring two more times before he fumbled for the phone where he'd tossed it on the nightstand. "'Lo."

"Kylen, this is Hansen. You awake?"

Kylen scrubbed one hand over his face and opened one eye just far enough to see the clock read 6:03 a.m. He released a sigh he hoped didn't sound too much like a moan to his boss. "I will be if you give me five minutes and a double-shot espresso."

Tom Hansen only grunted. "Sorry, I know your shift doesn't start for several hours yet, but this is important. I need you to get down to Sunset Beach right away. They've asked for a good man to help run some leads on a couple cases. I'm sending you."

"Sunset Beach. Sure. I can do that."

"Good. Pack a bag. I've offered you on loan to their department for two weeks until their new hire arrives from Maine."

Two weeks? Kylen flopped back against his

pillow. Layne needed some time. But not that much. Could he handle her thinking he was such a lowlife for two whole weeks? He'd have to. A phone call was not going to be the best way for them to iron this out. He'd wanted to give her some space. Just not quite that much. But maybe this would be better in the long run.

"Yes, sir." He hoped his boss didn't hear the defeat in his tone.

"Keep me updated."

"Yes, sir."

A week later Taysia pulled into the parking lot at Mom's Gym. She hurt all over. There was no other way to explain it. Not a physical pain. But a low, dull ache that originated in the region of her heart and spread all through her.

She shoved the car into park and stared across the road toward the pounding surf for a minute. The day was sunny, but it felt gray; warm, and yet a chill gripped her.

She hadn't heard from Kylen all week. Hadn't even caught a glimpse of him, even though she'd been back to staying at her own home for the past several nights, since Daddy seemed to be doing fine.

He had to have seen her note by now, so she'd obviously totally blown any chance she had with him.

With a sigh she pushed open her door and stepped out onto the walk, slinging her sports bag over her shoulder.

Sophia climbed out of the car next to her and stepped into her path.

Taysia froze. Great. Just who she'd been dying to see. What could she want now? She adjusted her bag. "Hi, Sophia."

Sophia folded her hands together and tapped her first fingers against her lips. She couldn't seem to meet Taysia's eyes, and tears glittered on her lower lids.

Taysia blinked. Tears were the last thing she'd expected from Sophia.

With a little huff, Sophia straightened her shoulders and lifted her chin. "I just wanted to say...sorry. I'm really sorry, Taysia. Kylen had nothing to do with that scene at the restaurant. It was all me."

Good thing the day was beautiful, because even a slight breeze could have knocked Taysia over at that moment. She never would have thought to see the day Sophia apologized to anyone. For anything. It took a moment before words would come, but finally she managed to stutter, "I-I know."

"Of course you do. The way Kylen tore out after you, you two probably had everything patched up that afternoon. I just wanted..." Her hands fluttered like she was seeking an elusive thought. "I *needed* to make things right."

Taysia worked the strap higher on her shoulder. Her heart melted a little at the pleading in Sophia's expression. "I appreciate that. Thank you."

Sophia met her gaze then. Her jaw dropped slightly, and she seemed to be searching Taysia's expression for something. "You are very gracious. I didn't expect that. Nor do I deserve it."

Well, if there wasn't proof miracles existed standing on the walk right in front of her, Taysia didn't know what else it might be. She cringed a little guiltily at the memory of her reaction to seeing Sophia a moment ago. *God, give me words. Open her eyes*. "None of us deserve grace, Sophia. I certainly didn't. But God gave it to me when I asked Him. So how can I give any less to those around me? I really do appreciate your change of heart. It means a lot." *But it likely won't bring Kylen back into my life*. Her shoulders slumped.

Sophia must have noticed her dejection, because she asked, "Kylen did find you that day, didn't he?"

Taysia forced words past the constriction in her throat. "Yes, he did. And I'm afraid I wasn't so gracious toward him." Tears threatened to overflow. She couldn't talk about this now. And especially not with Sophia, who she could so easily blame for all of it. She moved to pass the woman. "If you'll excuse me, I have classes starting in just a bit."

Sophia stepped out of the way. "Yes. Of

course." But before Taysia had gone more than two strides, she called, "Taysia?"

Taysia turned. "Yes?"

"Uh, I won't be, uh"—she waved a hand toward Mom's Gym—"pursuing my lawsuit."

Shocked speechless twice in one day—and by the same woman—who would have thought?

The next thing she knew, she was standing in the lobby of Mom's Gym staring at the car keys in her hand. She couldn't remember if she'd even offered a response to Sophia. She hoped she'd at least murmured some form of polite thanks. But try as she might, she couldn't recall.

Someone's sniffling penetrated her consciousness.

She straightened and shoved her keys into her purse, hurrying toward the front desk. "Marie? Is that you?"

Marie's head appeared above the counter. She was sitting in her desk chair but apparently had been leaning forward. "Oh, hi, Miss Green. I didn't hear you come in." Marie swiped at damp cheeks.

She's crying? "Marie?" Rounding the half wall that separated the lobby from the work space behind the counter, she scanned her young friend. "Are you okay?"

Marie's face crumpled, and she buried her face in her hands.

"Oh, honey." Taysia rested a comforting hand on her shoulder. "What is it?"

Marie just shook her head. For a long moment she remained silent. Her shoulders shook and tears dripped through her fingers.

Frowning in concern, Taysia snatched several tissues from the box on the desk and eased them under one of Marie's hands.

Marie clasped them and pressed them to her eyes, but held her silence.

A quick glance at her watch revealed she had to teach a class in less than thirty minutes. Women would start arriving soon. But Marie was in no condition to be working today. Still, she couldn't just shoo her out the door in her present state of mind. She squatted down by the girl and rubbed one of her shoulders. "Marie? What is it, honey? What's happened?"

"Oh, Taysia!" The words emerged more wail than statement. "I'm such an idiot!"

Taysia ground her teeth and reminded herself to be kind. It would be about a guy. It was always about a guy. Probably Kylen's cousin, Brice. She resisted a roll of her eyes. Marie would be better off without that young rake in her life. She took a fortifying breath and controlled her tone carefully. "If there's one thing I've learned about you over the past year, Marie, it's that you can do anything you put your mind to. I have no doubt it will be the same this time." She paused, but when Marie didn't offer even a morsel of information, she prodded, "You always feel better when you talk about things...what's happened?"

Marie squirmed in the chair. Then peeked at her above the edges of the now uselessly damp Kleenexes.

Taysia snatched four more from the box and held the garbage can toward her. After Marie deposited the others into the can, she handed her the clean tissues.

Marie sighed. Her face held about as much color as the white paper in the printer behind her.

Maybe she'd had more feelings for this guy than the others before him. Taysia folded her arms and waited, knowing Marie would figure out how to tell her eventually.

For a long moment, all Marie did was shred one of the tissues into little pills in her lap. Finally she glanced up and met Taysia's gaze for the briefest of seconds before she returned her attention to her little project. "I'm late."

The words were so soft, Taysia almost didn't hear them. She frowned and looked at her watch. Marie had gotten here before— With sudden clarity, the meaning of the words registered. Her eyes widened, and she sank onto her knees so she could peer into Marie's face. "How late?"

Marie sniffed. "Over a month."

"Did you take a test?"

The tiniest hint of a nod.

"And?"

Another nod. Another crumpling of her face, but she clenched her jaw this time and brought her expression back under control.

"Who's the father?"

Marie chewed the inside of her lip and suppressed another sob. "You're going to be so disappointed in me."

"Honey, just tell me."

"I don't know."

"You don't—" Taysia forced herself to stop talking before she said something she would really regret. Something that might ruin the fragile relationship she'd been building with the girl for the past few years.

"I know! I'm sorry! It could be any one of a number of guys. Most of whom have probably moved on by now. A couple months ago, right after Reece Cahill broke up with me, I spent several nights at Pete's trying to forget about him. There were a couple businessmen. And some guy with a Harley who was just passing through."

"Marie..." A sharp stab of pain shot right through Taysia's heart. She'd thought the girl had moved past that kind of behavior. "Could it be Reece's? Or Brice's?"

Marie's eyes widened and she shook her head. "No. Reece never...he's too good of a guy for that. And Brice and I, we never...no, it couldn't be his."

A sigh welled up from deep inside Taysia. "I see."

Marie's face contorted again. "I had an appointment last night at a...clinic."

Taysia's heart nearly dropped through the floor. Please God, she hadn't—

"But I couldn't go through with it. The words from the psalm you read to all your First Trimester Fitness classes about God knitting a baby together in its mother's womb kept running through my mind over and over. And I just...couldn't."

"Oh, honey." Taysia leaned forward and pulled Marie into a ferocious embrace. "I'm so glad you didn't—couldn't. We are going to make it through this. I'm going to be there for you every step of the way."

Marie sobbed into her shoulder, and Taysia remained right where she was, clutching the girl to her for a few more minutes. Conscious of the clock and the impending inundation of pregnant clients, Taysia finally eased back. She looked right into Marie's face. "Listen, now. Clients are going to start arriving soon, and you are in no condition to be here at work today." She grabbed her house keys out of her purse. "Why don't you run over to my place and just spend the day resting? Today's a short day, so I should be home just after noon, and we can talk more then, okay?"

Marie nodded, took the keys, and stood dejectedly to her feet.

"Oh, hon." Taysia gave her another quick hug. "Your life is not over, I promise. I'll see you at lunchtime, okay?"

With a little nod, Marie shuffled toward the door.

Taysia glanced at her watch again. Should she

cancel classes so she could spend the day with Marie? What if she tried to hurt herself? Or the baby? She was almost to the doors. "Marie?"

She turned.

"Would you like me to cancel classes and come with you now?"

Marie offered a sad smile and shook her head. "No. I'll be fine. I'm just a bit of an emotional mess. But it feels good to finally have told you. I'll go right to your place and wait for you. Don't worry. I'm going to be okay."

The rest of the week passed in a blur. Between teaching classes and running the front desk, Taysia spent all her free time helping Marie find a good obstetrician, speaking with Sophia's lawyers, who confirmed she'd dropped the case, and checking in on Daddy from time to time. Marie had stayed at her house all week, and they'd talked late into the night on several occasions.

By the time Friday rolled around, Taysia was exhausted. She pushed through the front door to her house and dropped her gym bag, leaving it where it fell. The good news was that Daddy and Loraine had planned to take a trip to Seaside tomorrow, so she could sleep in, guilt-free.

Marie popped her head out of the kitchen. "Oh, good, you're home. I made dinner, such as it is. But I think it's time for me to move back to my place, and I was hoping you could drive me tonight?"

Taysia suppressed a groan of weariness. She was glad to see some of Marie's spark returning. And it would be good for her to get back to her own place. Plus she'd made dinner. She forced a smile she hoped didn't droop too much around the edges. "Sure. I'm happy to drive you home. I'm glad to see you bouncing back a little." She pulled Marie into a hug and then released her. "What's for dinner?"

"Chicken and Caesar salad."

"Sounds delicious."

Marie stopped her with a hand to her arm. "Listen, Taysia. I really want to say thanks for all you've done for me. I know I've let you down, but you didn't turn your back on me, and for that I'll be forever thankful."

Taysia gripped Marie's shoulders and looked into her eyes. "I wouldn't turn my back on you for the world. We all make mistakes. And since there's no going back, only forward, it doesn't make a whole lot of sense to linger on those mistakes. We just ask for forgiveness from those we've wronged, and try to do better next time."

Tears sprang to Marie's eyes. "Will you forgive me?"

"Marie Sinclair, of course I forgive you. But I'm not the one you need to make amends with the most. Right?"

"Yeah, God. I know."

Taysia cupped a hand to the girl's cheek. "That's right. People may fail you—will fail you. But Jesus never will. Even when you fail Him. He's there with open arms saying, 'Get up. Try again. I'm not leaving.'"

"I love you so much!" Marie threw her arms around Taysia's neck and hugged her tight. "You're the first one who ever...stuck around, you know? After my mom left when I was thirteen and then Daddy went to prison, it was just me. Until you hired me. And...well, I have no words to say how much you mean to me."

Taysia squeezed her close and angled a glance at the ceiling. *Lord, help her to see Your love through me. She's really going to need it now.* To Marie she whispered, "That's what families do, Marie. They stick together. Now"—she set the girl at arm's length—"how about we eat? I'm starving!"

Chuckling, Marie swiped tears from beneath her eyes. "Me too."

Chapter 12

Taysia's car wasn't in her driveway and her house was all dark when Kylen arrived home Friday night. It was probably better she wasn't home, because he might have been tempted to go right over to talk with her. Where could she be?

He glanced at his watch. It was ten o'clock. Was she still staying at her dad's place?

He pushed through the garage door into the house and groaned when he saw the huge pile of mail lying on the floor in front of the main door.

After two weeks of late nights and terrible coffee, he was ready for some shut-eye. Thankfully they'd made an arrest in that abuse case just yesterday, so the new officer to Sunset Beach would have fairly smooth sailing on the case from here on out. And he'd seemed like a fairly competent guy.

He dropped his duffel bag by the laundry room door and glanced at the pile of mail again. First he would sleep. He could deal with the mail in the morning. He headed for his basement apartment and fell right to sleep, but at five thirty the next morning, the fact that he'd forgotten to close the blinds came back to bite him. The sunshine streaming in his window and the loud twittering of birds pulled him from the best night's rest he'd had in two weeks.

He groaned and sat up, knowing he'd never fall back to sleep. Besides, after being gone for two weeks, there were plenty of chores around the place to keep him busy. He pushed himself to his feet.

He might as well start with the mail.

The persistent ringing of the doorbell woke Taysia from a sound sleep. She leaped, bleary eyed, out of bed imagining all sorts of emergencies.

Daddy and Loraine...heading to Seaside. What if they'd gotten into a wreck?

She lurched toward the door. Her shoulder cracked against the frame on her way into the hall. "Ow!" *Eyes open. Eyes open!*

Marie...had something happened to Marie in the night?

She stubbed her toe on the coffee table. "Ow!" She scrambled over it.

What if Daddy'd had another stroke? Or something worse?

She fumbled with the lock, ripping a fingernail on the metal. "Ow!" She crammed the finger into her mouth as she yanked the door open.

Kylen stood on her porch, freshly showered, a latte in each hand, and looking better than any man had a right to.

She blinked. "What are you doing here?" Only then did she realize she'd spoken around her finger. She snatched it from her mouth, but that was when all the pain from every part of her body hit her. She gripped the doorframe and pressed her forehead into it.

"Layne?" His voice held a note of contrition and curiosity.

She couldn't just leave him standing on her porch...but she needed a moment to let the pain subside. Not just the pain from her klutzy rush to the door, but from two weeks of worrying and wondering, and now having him standing right here beside her.

"Are you okay?"

"Yes. I'm fine. I think." She forced herself upright and gestured him through to the living room, where she sank into the couch. Pressing one hand to her aching shoulder, she squinted at the clock. "Six? Kylen!" Leaning her head back, she closed her eyes with a groan.

He sank down next to her and bumped her gently with his shoulder. "I brought you coffee."

One eye peeked open, then shut again. She couldn't believe he was here. Sitting beside her. Acting like everything between them was normal. Truth be told, it was a good thing pain had made her head for the couch, because she didn't know if her legs would have held her upright.

Tingles of desire emanated from the spot on her shoulder he'd just touched. Desire to press close to him and never pull away. She swallowed down the urge and held her silence, reminding herself she didn't know why he was actually here.

"Tall vanilla macchiato, skinny, no whip, just like you like it."

Yes, she could surely use a jolt of caffeine right now. She held out one hand.

He chuckled, but she felt the warmth of the paper cup settle into her palm. A fortifying sip sent a surge of contentment through her. "Mmmm. I could almost forgive you for waking me up before the birds and scaring the living daylights out of me."

"The birds are up. They are what woke me and made me go read my mail." His words were warm and thick with emotion.

Her pulse skittered. Had he just now gotten around to seeing her note? She was dying to know where he'd been for the past couple weeks. But instead of asking, she forced a grumble of joviality into her tone. "Surely it's way too early for the birds to be awake."

He chuckled.

She wasn't ready to hear his answers to her questions yet, so she lifted her foot, eyes still sealed. "Is my toe bleeding?"

The couch jostled as he knelt down and captured her foot to examine it. "No. Why?" His fingers began a slow massage along the side of her foot.

A jolt traversed her leg, and she curled her French-tip toes.

"Because I almost took it off rushing for the door."

"I'm sorry." He hesitated, then added, "You said, 'scaring the daylights out of you.' Why? What's happened?"

She sighed. "That is a long story, better left for when I'm more awake."

His fingers worked the taut tendons of her ankle. "I should have called you instead of ringing the bell."

Raising the cup of coffee, she said, "All is forgiven."

Fingers barely missing a beat, he didn't answer, just kept massaging her foot. The silence stretched so long Taysia knew he was questioning whether her statement held a deeper meaning. Finally, she forced herself to look at him.

Oooh, boy. That was a mistake.

His dark eyes studied her intently, the black of his T-shirt only making them more forceful. She should look away—*needed* to look away, but like a powerful magnet, his gaze held hers captive.

His thumbs left the arch of her foot, where he'd massaged deep circles. He took the coffee cup from her hands and set it on the coffee table as he sat down on the couch beside her again. He leaned toward her, a glint in his gaze.

She had plenty of time to pull away if she wanted to. But the desire to do so had fled from her arsenal of self-preservation.

His shoulder connected with hers; his eyes dropped to her mouth.

Pulse racing like a marathon runner, she moistened her lips, and heaven help her, she wanted nothing more than to give in. But first she needed to hear his side of the story. “Kylen, I’m sorry. I never should have doubted you. Please, tell me your side of what happened.”

Relief seemed to sap his strength and rigidity. He collapsed forward and pressed his forehead against hers. “Sophia must have seen you coming. She said she’d be right back, and then the next thing I knew, she’d fallen into my lap and laid that kiss on me, and you were tearing back out of there.”

“She came and talked to me at the gym. She apologized and dropped the suit.”

He jolted back a bit. “She did?”

“I was surprised too.” Taysia nodded. “But she really seemed to mean it.”

Kylen sighed. “Well, that’s something, I guess.”

Taysia swallowed. “I’m so sorry, Ky. I should have stay—”

His thumb settled over her lips as he cupped her face. He shook his head. His gaze, so close and full of concern, never left hers. “We both know I’d given you plenty of reasons in the past to doubt me. We have lots of waves in our history, Layne. But I'm hoping it will be smooth sailing from here on out."

She couldn't disguise the concern that puckered her brow. "It's been two weeks, Ky. I thought you—that you—well, that I had ruined everything. Where have you been?"

He grimaced. "I'm sorry. Sunset Beach. They needed an extra man for a couple weeks, and Captain Hansen sent me." His thumb stroked her cheek ever so softly. "I didn't think a phone call or email was the best way to deal with the way we left things. And of course I didn't know that you had figured things out. Even if you hadn't written me that note, I planned to track you down and make you see reason the minute I got home. But you were out last night when I arrived."

"You must have gotten here when I was taking Marie home."

"Marie was here? Friday night girls' night?"

She sighed. Now was as good a time to tell him as any. "No. Marie stayed with me for a few days this week."

"Oh? Something happen to her place?"

"No." She pinned him with a look and then had to glance away and blink back tears. "She's pregnant, Ky. She needed someone with her to help her think through the future."

"She's—" Tension zipped through him. "Is it Brice's?"

Taysia pinched the bridge of her nose. "I don't

think so. She at least says it couldn't be him. In fact, she says she doesn't know who the father is."

Concern etched his features. "Is she going to be alright?"

Taysia thought for a long moment, then finally answered, "I hope so. She's strong. She's had to be. But I can tell she's really scared. She's chosen to keep the baby, though, and I'm really thankful for that."

"That's good. We'll need to be there for her. She's going to need all the support she can get."

Taysia flopped her head back against the couch and then rolled it toward him. Love for the man threatened to overwhelm her. "Kylen, forgive me? For running off and not trusting you? I need to hear you say it."

He leaned over and kissed her softly, then eased away just enough to cradle her cheek in one palm. "I forgive you, Taysia. Truth is, I was so hurt that you assumed the worst that I didn't respond very well. So...forgive me for not just saying straight out what really happened?"

This time she kissed him. "I forgive you. Not that I was in any sort of emotional state to have listened."

Humor crinkled the corners of his eyes as he leaned forward and lingered over another kiss. "This forgiveness thing could really work to a guy's benefit. Let's see...what else can I ask you to forgive me for...?"

She chuckled and thumped his chest with the

back of her hand. But she didn't protest when he leaned in again. His lips settled on hers more firmly this time. Tugging. Pulling. Parting. And as his tongue caressed hers, she wrapped her arms around his neck and freed all the passion and emotion that had been dammed up for the past two weeks. Her fingers curled into the hair at the back of his head, and she pressed herself closer to him.

"Layne." The word emerged on a groan as he snatched his hands from her waist and thrust them behind his back. He pressed his forehead to hers, his eyes closed, his breaths coming rapidly. Then he leaned in and gave her a quick final kiss before he leapt to his feet and reached down a hand for her. "Come jogging with me?"

She heaved in a shuddering breath and allowed him to help her to her feet. Jogging was the last thing on her mind, but he was right. They needed to get out into public. Her gaze traveled to his lips. She wanted more. And she could see the same desire reflected in his eyes. The power of her desire scared her a little. She wanted him so much that if she gave in to the need, she might not stop. They both stepped back from each other at the same moment, and she chuckled tremulously. "Yeah, jogging's probably a really good idea."

He took another exaggeratedly large step back and grinned at her.

She was once more overwhelmed with how

much he cared for her. The fact that he was putting his own desires on hold, and encouraging her to do the same because it was the right thing to do, only made her love him more.

He stopped at her door and rubbed his thumb over his lips as though the feeling of their kiss still lingered there. "I'll go get changed and meet you outside?"

"Yeah." She nodded and willed down the trembling caused by the adrenaline rush. "See you out there."

Taysia changed into a white spandex top and running shorts and slipped into her favorite running shoes. She took time to put up her hair so she wouldn't have to fight it in the notorious Pacific wind, and added a little makeup. By the time she finally got herself together enough to head for the beach, she was sure Kylen would be waiting for her. But when she arrived at the place they normally started their jog from, he still wasn't anywhere to be seen.

She turned to glance back in the direction of their houses, and stilled. The sunrise was so spectacular, Taysia drew in a breath of awe. She absentmindedly pulled up one quad to stretch as she studied the sky above their rooftops. Shards of coral and watermelon pink shot through with lemon yellow swirled with every shade of purple imaginable before fading to lavender, peach, and cream above her head.

She heard Kylen's footsteps crunching in the sand as she switched to stretch out her other leg, but just then a flock of gulls cavorting against the backdrop of the sunrise drew her attention. "Isn't it beautiful?" she asked, unable to disguise the awe in her voice.

"Yes." It was the husky quality of that one little word that shot a dart of awareness through her. Dropping her foot, she turned to face him.

He was wearing a suit and tie. And carrying a huge bouquet of her favorite purple lupines that grew wild along the beach this time of year interspersed with beach grass. The bouquet was large enough to almost be a burden. But it was the glint in his eye that sent her heart rate soaring. A glint that held a note of mischief, promise, hope, and adoration.

"You can't go jogging in a suit..." Her hands flew to her mouth. He couldn't be... "Kylen!?"

He grinned and held out the bouquet to her.

She took the flowers reflexively, resting them against the crook of one arm as she studied his expression.

It turned oh so serious as he took her hand and dropped to one knee on the sand before her.

Everything in her went still.

"Anastaysia Layne Green"—he tilted his head, his eyes never leaving her face—"will you marry me?"

The strength left her legs, and she dropped to her knees before him. Slowly, she set the bouquet of lupines onto the sand. Wrapping her arms around his neck, she pressed her forehead to his and just took in the moment. She pulled in a slow breath. She was so undeserving of this man, of this moment of happiness, of the lifetime promised to them. Yet here it was being offered, and with love at that.

Pulling back just slightly, she caressed his cheek with the backs of her fingers and then met his gaze.

His brows arched, and he worked one side of his lip like his life depended on it.

"I might not be the perfect wife."

He chuckled. "I know I won't be the perfect husband."

Her heart thundered a staccato beat against her sternum. "We have a lot of mistakes in our past...do you think we can—"

He laid a finger over her lips. "'But one thing I do: Forgetting what is behind and straining toward what is ahead, I press on toward the goal to win the prize for which God has called me heavenward in Christ Jesus.' Philippians chapter three, thirteen and fourteen. We have a lot of mistakes, Layne, yes. But we have to put that behind us and move forward. And with God's help, we can do that."

Tears blurred her vision. Hadn't she just been pondering those verses a few days ago? Yes, God would help them. Love for the man threatened to overwhelm her. Leaning forward, she pressed a light kiss to his lips, then whispered, "You're right."

"So? What do you say?"

"Yes. Yes. A thousand times yes."

He grinned. Kissed her quickly. Then gave a loud whoop and leapt to his feet, pulling her with him. He swung her around and around, laughing like a crazy man.

She giggled and struggled for her freedom. "Put me down, Kylen Sumner, before I change my mind!"

"Oh no you don't!" He set her on her feet and draped his arms lazily against her shoulders. His breaths came in short puffs as he bent down and grinned into her face. "No changing your mind allowed. You are stuck with me now."

"Well..." She grabbed his tie and rose on her tiptoes to give him a quick peck. "I think I can live with that."

Epilogue

The day of the wedding dawned bright and sunny. Taysia woke with the sunrise and rushed through breakfast before hurrying out the door to meet Loraine and Marie at the hairdresser's.

As she drove, she pondered the last few hectic weeks.

Even though Loraine and Daddy had married in a very spur-of-the-moment ceremony several weeks back, Taysia hadn't quite been able to bring herself to call Loraine Mom yet. But the woman had stepped into the mothering role like she'd been doing it all her life, and today's hair appointments had been set up at her insistence. Taysia really was looking forward to a bit of pampering. Heaven knew she could use it after the last few weeks of planning for the wedding and trying to keep her business running, to boot.

Yes, Loraine was a special woman and had done amazing things for Daddy's disposition, lately including getting the man to church. Last week, when Loraine and Daddy had walked into the Wednesday night Bible study class, Taysia had nearly fallen off her seat. Daddy had shrugged and dismissed her questioning with "Kylen invited us, and Loraine said we should come."

Kylen had winked at her from behind Daddy's back.

Now, as Taysia pulled into a parking spot in front of the hairdresser's, she grinned and shook her head at the memory. She would keep praying and reminding herself that God loved Daddy and Loraine more than she could ever even imagine loving them.

Marie was standing on the walk by the door waiting for her. Her tummy was just starting to round now that she was in her fifth month, and Taysia was once again reminded of God's goodness and love.

Marie had finally and truly given her life to the Lord a couple months back, and she'd been like a new person ever since. Her maturity and care for others had really blossomed over the past few weeks, and Taysia didn't know if she would have been able to pull this wedding off if it wasn't for Marie's help. She knew she and Kylen wouldn't be headed for Hawaii tomorrow if it wasn't for the fact that Marie had really stepped up and would be running the gym for those two weeks.

At first, she'd been a bit worried. But she found, now that the time to leave was here, she didn't have any concerns. Marie would do a fine job for all the clients.

She hugged the girl, who gave a little squeal and then set her back at arm's length. "Are you ready for this, Taysia?"

A grin as large as the Cheshire's bloomed. "Oh, you better believe I'm ready!"

The pampering at the hairdresser's was just as lovely as she'd counted on it being, and two hours later she was standing at the head of the aisle with her arm looped through Daddy's.

Marie looked radiant in the purple gown they'd settled on. And Brice, who Kylen had chosen to stand up with him, tugged at the sleeves of his black tux.

The flowers, a mixture of purple lupines (that they'd had to buy from a hothouse because the ones on the beach were out of season now) and white roses, looked amazing. And several lit candles added to the beauty of the moment.

But it was Kylen who she couldn't tear her gaze from. Kylen who was waiting for her at the front of the church—in front of all their friends and family. Kylen who would be her partner and companion, lover and friend, for the rest of her life.

He looked so handsome in his tux and white vest.

She grinned as she remembered trying to talk him into wearing a purple vest. But he'd wanted nothing to do with that and had given her a flat-out no followed by a kiss.

His dark gaze gleamed with satisfaction when

he found her at the head of the aisle, and his feet shuffled as though anticipation made it impossible for him to stand still. The music started, and as she and Daddy stepped slowly down the aisle, everyone stood. She lost sight of Kylen for a moment. But when he reappeared, they were only steps from each other.

Her breath caught. How could one man be so handsome? He was perfect, this man made for her, even if she did miss his usual five o'clock shadow.

Daddy gave her away with a hitch in his voice, and she lifted her veil far enough to give him a kiss on the cheek. And then she was *there*. Standing beside the man she'd loved since a long-ago summer under a willow tree. Pledging herself to him until her dying day and hearing his sweet words of promised commitment in return.

And when the minister finally said, "You may kiss your bride," she felt like every joy in the world burst to life inside her.

Kylen's hands trembled as he lifted the veil back from her face. Then he cupped her neck with one hand and whispered softly, "We did it."

"Yes," she whispered back. "And I couldn't be happier."

"Me either." He kissed her then as though they weren't standing in front of a crowd of people. As though he might never get the chance to kiss her again and needed to store up a bank of emotions and feelings. Finally, when the audience started to titter, he eased back and grinned at her. "I love you, Mrs. Sumner," he breathed.

After that kiss she wasn't sure her legs would sustain her up the aisle. And she was glad for the moment of reprieve the cheers from the audience provided as she looped her arm through Kylen's and they turned to face their friends and family. Kylen pumped his fist in the air, bringing even more whistles and cheers, and Taysia couldn't withhold a laugh.

She glanced over at Kylen, her face stretched in a mile-wide smile. *Thank You, God, for bringing this man back into my life. Help me to love him and remain faithful to him always. I can't wait to see what the future holds. And I know You are going to be with us every wonderful step of the way.*

And she did. She really did.

After all, He'd brought them this far. Beyond the waves of sin and uncertainty, doubt and fear. And onto the sea of His love and desire for their lives. There would probably still be storms ahead, but they would weather them together. With God's help.

Excerpt from *Caught in the Current*, Pacific Shores, Book 2 Available Now

Chapter 1

"Alyssa Anne Sinclair, you come back here right now!" Marie dashed down the cereal aisle after her precocious three-and-a-half-year-old.

"But Mommy, I want the chocate kind. Wif mashmallows." Alyssa stopped directly in front of a box at kid-eye-level with enough cartoon characters on it to start a new animation network.

Marie sighed and squatted down next to her daughter. Running one hand over her little one's disarrayed hair, she pondered several things all at once. First, how did Alyssa's hair always end up in so many tangles only an hour into the day? Second, how was she going to talk her out of the chocolate cereal that should come standard with a vial of insulin? And third, and certainly not least, what was she going to do if she couldn't find a sitter?

She certainly couldn't afford to take time off of work. And Taysia was already much too kind to her when it came to taking time away from the gym to be with Alyssa. The problem was, she'd known for several months that Mrs. Hernandez was moving to Arizona to live near her daughter. Just...procrastination had gotten the better of her – again. Now she had a week to figure this out or she'd be forced to request time off.

Beside her Alyssa pooched out her lower lip and gave her a good dose of the best pleading expression she could apparently muster. Marie bit back a grin. She had to have a heart of stone because the look wasn't doing much for her.

"Honey, I know Aunt Taysia and Uncle Kylen let you have that kind sometimes when you go to their house, but it's really not good for you. Mom grabbed you the crunchy kind with raspberries that you like so much." She resisted the urge to stick her tongue into her cheek and prayed Alyssa would fall for it.

"But I only like that kind when the chocate kind isn't in the cupboard."

"Well." Marie stood and tried another tactic. "I'm sorry, but I don't have enough money to buy both, so we have to leave this one here today." She cringed, knowing how ineffective that argument would be since her three-year-old had no understanding of income versus expense.

"But mommy!" Big tears pooled on Alyssa's lower lids.

Oh boy, here we go. "Hey, how about if we go pick out some yogurt for you to pack in your lunches this week, Super Woman?"

"Yogurt! Yum!" With one blink, and not even a

telephone booth in site, the transformation from pout to glee was complete, and Alyssa dashed down the aisle.

Swinging the cart around, Marie called, "Wait for me, sweetheart. And no running in the store please."

Alyssa obediently slowed to the fastest "walk" she could possibly muster.

Yogurt. Who knew? Marie tucked that little weapon into her mommy-arsenal for future reference.

Alyssa disappeared around the end of the aisle and Marie picked up the pace, even though she wasn't really worried. Marinville was a fairly small, quiet town, and almost everyone knew and loved Alyssa who'd never known a stranger.

But before her cart had even reached the main section by the yogurts, there came the loud crash of breaking glass, a masculine grunt, and a three-year-old gasp.

Marie cringed to a halt, and held her breath, sure more damage loomed. She could envision a whole end-cap display crashing to the ground.

Thankfully, only Alyssa's voice broke the silence. "Uh-oh! Sorry!"

Alyssa did sound truly sorry but that didn't ease the stone of dread that dropped into Marie's stomach. Whatever had just broken sounded expensive and she was going to have to pay for it. Why hadn't she insisted Alyssa sit in the cart, like a normal mother would have?

Well, the only thing to do was to go see what had happened. She started forward.

"Hey there, Super Woman. I'm sorry – I should have been watching where I was going more carefully, I guess."

Marie jerked the cart to a stop with such force her stack of soup cans toppled.

That voice. It couldn't be! Her heart lodged in her throat, and she prayed Alyssa would come looking for her so she could go down the aisle the other way and not have to face the man currently talking to her daughter. Maybe it wasn't really him? She froze and listened with all her might.

"Hey!" Alyssa's tone was indignant. "How did you know I am Super Woman?"

Marie heard the sound of glass tinking together and some scuffling like he was using his foot to scoot the shattered shards into a pile. "Well, by the big S on your pink shirt, I guess."

"You're tall."

The man chuckled. And a sweet sensation like a drizzle of honey on sour dough toast settled into the pit of Marie's stomach. How long had it been since she'd heard that oh so familiar, gentle laugh? *Reece Cahill*. Marie's eyes dropped closed.

"I guess I am tall, now that you mention it." A boot squeaked on the tiles, and this time when Reece spoke his voice seemed to be coming to her from a drastically de-elevated level. "How's that? Better?"

"You have eyes like grass. My mommy likes

grass eyes."

Reece's chuckle again, full of curiosity this time. "Grass eyes?"

"You know, the color of grass."

"Oh!" Reece's boots squeaked on the tiles again. "Speaking of your Mommy—" his voice emerged slightly muffled this time— "is she around here someplace, tyke?"

Marie jolted into action. Great. Now he would think she was a terrible mother who couldn't even keep track of one little girl, on top of all the other things he already knew about her. She forced one foot in front of the other and rolled her cart out into the open.

Reece squatted on the balls of his feet before Alyssa. His typical attire of cowboy boots, jeans, t-shirt and Stetson hadn't changed over the years, she noted. What had changed was his lankiness. The man was no longer tall and straight. He was tall and...chiseled. There was no other way to put it. He'd always been strong and athletic, but now...muscles stretched his t-shirt in all the right places to mouthwatering degrees.

She swallowed and focused on her daughter, who stood right in front of the man with his cheeks cupped in her chubby hands as she closely – very closely – examined his eyes. Eyes Marie well remembered, and likely the reason green was her favorite color.

Reece must have caught site of her shoes, because he tipped his head ever so slightly and peered around her daughter. His gaze started at her grimy, Saturday-chore tennis shoes and traveled all the way up past her jogging shorts and paint splattered t-shirt to her face.

His eyes rounded. "Marie!" He stood slowly, reflexively picking up Alyssa and settling her on one very sinewy forearm. He pushed his hat back on his head and swept a glance from her head to ankles and back again. Then he looked from her to Alyssa, a light of understanding dawning on his face. His focus dropped to where her ringless left hand rested on the handle of the shopping cart.

Marie's face flamed so hot it likely could have sizzled bacon. Yeah, he probably wouldn't be surprised to note she still wasn't married. "Hi Reece. I'm really sorry about all this." She swiped a gesture to the three jars of pickles broken open by his feet. "Just tear off the bar codes and I'll pay for them when I get to the front."

Oh boy... She resisted the urge to cringe, and really hoped that didn't sound like she'd done this before half a dozen times...or so. She chanced a glance at his face.

But Reece's attention had zoned in on her daughter, his head pulled back to make focusing on Alyssa's face easier. "You're an old pro at this, huh?"

Alyssa shrugged. "Mommy says my feet move faster than my brain sometimes."

To his credit Reece withheld the bark of laughter Marie could tell wanted to burst forth.

He only nodded sagely. "You know, I think my feet did a lot of going faster than my brain when I was your age too."

"Really?" Alyssa swung a look her way. "Mommy, he broke pickles too!"

Marie smiled but all she really wanted to do was escape from the presence of the only man she'd ever had any real feelings for. From the only man who'd ever broken her heart. She stretched a hand out to her daughter. "Come on, Super Woman, we need to go find someone to clean this up. Then we need to grab your yogurt and get back home."

Reece complied with her unspoken request, and put Alyssa on the floor. Marie took her little convict's hand in a firm grip.

"Nice to see you again," she offered in parting and hurried to make her escape.

But as she started to lead Alyssa away her daughter stiffened and hung back. "Mommy, we have to get the scanny things so we can pay."

"Right."

Drat. No chance for escape yet.

"And I don't want to do dishes this time. That was no fun."

Marie pressed her lips together and didn't meet Reece's gaze. He was still standing stock still, his hands resting on slim hips. He probably thought she and Alyssa had come here straight from the loony bin. "Well...you have to do something to work off your debt. We've talked about running in the store lots of times. This," she held a hand out to the spreading puddle of pickle juice, "is what happens when you do." She was trying to tamp down her irritation and keep her words loving, but as if it wasn't bad enough that Alyssa had done something like this again, it had to have been Reece!

She squatted next to the mess of pickles and glass.

Where had he been for all these years, anyway? She hadn't seen him since...when? Four years at least. She'd still been pregnant with Alyssa when she'd heard he'd left town and no one seemed to know where he'd gone off to.

As she found the shards of the jars with the barcodes and worked to pull one of them free, she noticed that he'd been buying some sort of organic, all-natural pickles. Of course he had. Because Alyssa couldn't have run into someone who was buying just one jar of the el-cheapo store brand. Why was he buying 3 jars of pickles anyhow? This was probably going to cost her at least fifteen bucks after tax. She mentally recalculated what was already in the cart that she could return to the shelf.

Reece was suddenly squatting by her side. "Listen, this really wasn't all her fault. I was carrying three jars of these things, and if I hadn't left my cart over there by the cold foods section the jars never would have fallen. Why don't you let me cover it just this once?"

Just his nearness and the sound of his voice were doing things to her pulse that could set off all sorts of alarms if she were hooked up to a monitor. She kept her focus on the floor, not daring to meet his eyes. "No. No. I couldn't let you do that. If she hadn't been running, your pickles would have made it to your cart just fine."

Why was this sticker being so stubborn about coming off the glass? The thing was soaked in pickle juice; if anything that should help it come loose easier.

"Your daughter is beautiful." His words were low and raspy.

That did it. She stood and tucked a strand of hair behind her ear. "Thank you. Nice seeing you again. Alyssa, come on honey." She would just take the whole broken piece to the register and tell them to ring up three of them.

Reece rose with her. "Marie..." his tone said she was being stubborn.

Well that may be, but she wasn't about to let him pay for Alyssa's rambunctiousness. She chose to ignore his chiding. And the fact that he hadn't taken his gaze off her face for the past several minutes.

Alyssa had ignored her call and squatted next to a seep of pickle juice. Chubby hands resting against little knees, she scooted along with it, following the trickling green river as it expanded across the tiles.

As Marie reached to set the broken jar into the

child seat on the cart, her peripheral vision caught one chubby hand reaching toward a shard of glass. "Alyssa! Don't touch that! I don't want you getting cut." She glanced over to ensure her daughter was going to listen, but doing so made her hand miss the seat. Her grip slipped on the juice-greased glass. With a jolt she tried to catch it. She felt the sharp slice of pain angle across the pad of her finger and over one knuckle. She hissed and reflexively dropped the piece of the jar, which shattered it into several more shards.

Reece was immediately by her side.

She had instinctively clamped the fingers of her other hand around the injury.

He reached for it. "Let me see." He stepped so close his hat-brim brushed her cheek when he leaned forward to look at the cut. His touch was gentle and probably meant to be soothing.

But her heart had apparently received some sort of errant signal, because it was beating fast enough to count as aerobic exercise.

A low sound of distress rumbled in his throat. "This is pretty deep. I think you are going to need stitches."

Sure, that was just what she needed. A doctor bill.

She snatched her hand from his grasp. "I'll be fine, I'm sure. Nothing a Band-Aid won't fix."

She examined her finger. A flap of skin gaped open and blood was already dripping on the floor. The glass had somehow managed to slice down the side of her finger also. Oh boy. That cut was a doozey. Old familiar words that used to be part of her everyday vocabulary sprang to mind, and she clamped her teeth shut before any of them could pop out. But she had to do something. What? "Ah. Okay." She couldn't seem to think. *Do not panic. Do not panic*.

She'd never been too good around the sight of blood, though she'd gotten a little better at handling it now that she was a single mother of an accident prone toddler.

They really could not go to the hospital. Her insurance only covered 70% of emergency room visits, and she couldn't even afford an extra dollar in her budget right now, much less who-knew-how-much.

Plus she had things she needed to get done. Tomorrow was her day to bring the weekly treat for their Sunday School class, so she needed to get her cinnamon rolls baked. And she had a second coat of paint to put on the last wall of the unit next door for Mr. Meyer, her apartment complex manager, before she earned the extra hundred bucks she needed to pay all her bills this month.

She needed...Band-Aids. She glanced at the injury again. Okay, butterfly Band-Aids. A wave of light headedness drained through her.

Marie turned a sickly pale greenish color. "Whoa." Reece's stomach clenched and he lurched toward her and gripped both of her shoulders. He bent down and peered into her face. "Take a breath, Marie."

She complied.

"Good. And another." This time he let go of her shoulders and took hold of her cut hand, clamping his own fist around the now severely bleeding digit. "Alyssa," he snapped his fingers at the little girl who was apparently engrossed in the moving green liquid. "How would you like to take a ride with me and your mom in my big blue truck?"

Alyssa leapt to her feet. "Yes!"

Good. Looked like he'd pegged her right. Always up for a new adventure just like her mother was. His gaze skittered back to Marie. *Or at least used to be.*

She still looked like she was about to hurl. Maybe she didn't like doctors? "A few stitches and you'll be as good as new."

"Reece, I really can't—"

But just then the box-boy stepped into view.

Reece cut her off and called, "Excuse me?"

The kid, who had to be about sixteen, stepped over, his eyes widening as he took in the chaos surrounding them.

Reece gestured from the drips of blood around their feet to the splat of pickles and glass in the aisle. "Could you clean this up for us, please? And put that grocery cart there—" he pointed to his groceries down by the cold stuffs— "and this cart here—" he pointed to hers— "off to the side somewhere? I'll be back to get it all in about an hour."

The kid scratched his head and examined the mess, his eyes darting from the pickles to the blood and back again, as though wondering which disaster to clean up first.

Marie cringed. "I'm really sorry, Alex."

Reece's eyebrows went up. She obviously knew the kid. How many times had the poor guy had to clean up after them? He fleetingly wondered how many other mothers in the world were on a first-name basis with the clean-up crew at their grocery stores.

But Alex didn't seem fazed. "Oh don't worry Miss Sinclair. We employees sort of had a bet—" His eyes shot wide and he spun on one heel, making a hasty retreat as he called over one shoulder, "Don't worry, I'll clean it up, and yeah, I'll have the carts waiting for you, sir."

Reece grinned down at her. "I think Alyssa might have just made that boy some money."

"How nice that my daughter's accident-proneness can be fodder for an excellent gaming economy at Thrift and Save." Marie's face turned the prettiest shade of pink he'd seen in a long time. Her hand felt fragile under his. She was still as small and delicate as he remembered.

He swallowed. Four years of running from his feelings for her and his first full day back in town he met her at the grocery store. What were the odds? Maybe God was trying to tell him something? She wasn't wearing a ring—he gave himself a mental shake. A woman like her would certainly have a man in her life. And it was best he remember that.

Get back to the business at hand. He almost rolled his eyes at the inadvertent pun. "We should go."

"Listen. I don't need a doctor. Just a Band-Aid." She looked a trifle terrified at the thought of going to the hospital.

Reece's eyes narrowed. He didn't want to scare her further, but he'd definitely seen the white of bone where the cut had crossed over her knuckle.

Her chin lifted in an oh-so-familiar stubborn tilt.

Then again, maybe giving her a good dose of reality was the only way to get her to do what was needed. He shook his head. "Band-Aid's not going to be enough. You need a doctor. The cut is really deep. And do you know how many germs could be on that glass? It was on the floor before it cut you. Besides, the way that looked, you could have cut a tendon. You need to have it looked at."

Marie ran her free hand back through her hair. Her finger, still firmly in Reece's grasp was throbbing to beat the band, and despite his death hold on it, blood still seemed to be leaking out. She probably did need a doctor. She dropped her free hand to her side in frustration. She would just have to try and find a couple more odd jobs this month. "Fine."

"That's my girl."

Marie's heart did a double flip. Of course he hadn't meant the words to be anything more than encouragement. But the feel of his warm fingers around hers was much too enjoyable even if he was only trying to keep her from bleeding to death. She didn't want her heart following that current again. It was nothing but a riptide that could tear her apart.

"Here, just..." she grabbed up the hem of her t-shirt and indicated he should let go of her finger. The second he let go, blood seeped into the space and started to drip on the floor again. She clamped a wad of her t-shirt around it. She offered him a flick of a glance. "We better take my car. I don't want to get blood all over your truck."

Reece pushed out his lower lip, wiped his bloody palm on his jeans, and snagged a set of keys from his front pocket. "No worries."

She darted a glance at her purse. "Could you..." Before she could figure out exactly what she wanted him to do with it, he'd picked it up and looped the strap around her neck, angling it across her body so it settled against one hip.

"Good?" He was so close she could see the flecks of amber in his irises.

Mouth dry, she nodded.

"Let's just take my truck. It will be easier for

me just to drive you. Besides, I already promised Alyssa here a ride, didn't I, kid? You ready to go?" He squatted down to floor level. "Hop onto my back and we'll take your mom to get her finger looked at."

"I love piggy back rides!" Alyssa gave a little squeal and clambered aboard.

As he stood, Reece gave a distinct whinny. He snagged his Stetson from his head and plopped it back onto Alyssa's curls, then leapt a couple of trots ahead. "No pigs around here. Only horses."

Marie shook her head and followed them down the aisle at a much more sedate pace.

Alyssa giggled and used one hand to push back the much too large hat. "You're funny. Do you want to be my daddy?"

Marie stumbled.

Chapter 2

Thankfully Marie caught herself before she sprawled flat right there in the main aisle. But if ever she'd wanted the floor to open up and swallow her, this was it.

Reece only let out a bark of laughter and spun around to walk backwards, assessing her with glimmering green eyes. "You don't have a daddy, huh?"

While he'd directed the question at her daughter, there was a simmering curiosity in his gaze that flooded Marie with heat.

"Nope. Mr. Jackson wants to be my daddy, and Mommy said "maybe." But he's not—"

"—Alyssa!"

Blessedly, for once in her life, Alyssa seemed to catch onto the fact that Marie didn't want her to share further, and she let the rest of whatever she'd planned to say drop.

A breath of relief pushed past Marie's lips. But just to ensure something like this never happened again, she focused a mother-eye on Alyssa. "That is not a question you are to ask a man again – ever – do you understand?"

"But Mommy, why? I think he would be a fun daddy, don't you?"

"No!"

Reece winced and jammed a fist over his heart as though holding onto the handle of a knife she'd just thrust there.

Marie resisted a smile at his theatrics. "Well...maybe."

Reece's eyebrows shot up.

She hurried on before he could comment. "But that's not how getting a daddy works."

Oh boy, this was a mess. Had she really just said maybe? And right after Alyssa had mentioned Dan? Reece was going to think she hadn't changed a smidge since he broke up with her in high school.

Reece was having just a bit too much fun with this. He tucked his lower lip between his teeth, squinched up his face, and tilted his head, as though seriously assessing her answer. Then she noted the glimmer of amusement crinkling the corners of his eyes.

The man was laughing at her predicament! She wrinkled her nose at him.

He grinned and, after a quick wink, faced forward again.

She couldn't deny her relief at being free from his scrutiny.

Alyssa had apparently been pondering her response, because just then she piped up with, "How does getting a daddy work then?"

Reece gave a distinct snort, but mercifully he didn't turn to look at her this time.

The automatic sliding doors opened for them, and they stepped out into the warm July heat of the Pacific coast. Maybe she could just change the subject. "We'll need to get Alyssa's car-seat from my car."

Reece seemed to take pity on her and joined in the effort. "Sure. Where are you parked?"

She gestured as best she could with her t-shirt compressed finger toward her ancient, rust-marbled white Toyota Corolla. And of course the keys were in her purse. She fumbled with trying to keep the compression on her finger and lift the flap on her purse at the same time.

"Here, let me." Reece stepped close, but then paused. "Do you mind?"

It wasn't like she was going to have an easy time getting the keys out herself. She might as well complete her lesson in humiliation and get it over with. She shook her head. "Go ahead. Thanks."

As Reece set to digging through her purse, she considered their driving situation again. "We really should just take my car. We'll have to come right back by here on our way home from the hospital, and I can just drop you off at your truck, and then we won't have to transfer the car seat back and forth."

"But Mommy! I want to ride in the big blue truck!"

Reece scrunched one eye closed and offered her an apologetic look, even as he lifted her keys on one finger. "Tell you what, kiddo." He swung Alyssa down to the pavement and bent to look into her face.

Marie loved the way he got right down to Alyssa's level when he communicated with her. Something went soft inside her.

"How about we go get your mom's finger fixed up at the hospital, then we come back here to get groceries, and then you and your mom can ride in my truck to the welcome home barbeque my parents are hosting for me tonight?" He angled a questioning look at her over his shoulder.

"Yes! Yes! Yes!" Alyssa was already clapping her hands and jumping up and down.

All the softness Marie had just been feeling hardened into granite. How could she say "no" when he'd just gotten Alyssa's hopes so high? But she really must say no. She still had so much to get done. "No, I'm sorry. We can't. Can we just..." She let the words trail away and blinked hard at the asphalt under her feet. All she really wanted to do was go back home and crawl into bed and sleep for several hours. But that was not going to happen.

Exhaustion pressed down on her. She'd already worked five eight-hour shifts at the gym this week, plus put in several hours after Alyssa was asleep each night painting the apartment across the hall for her landlord just to get a hundred bucks.

If Reece wasn't careful, he was going to end up with one very emotional female to deal with.

"Please, mommy? Please? Please? Please?!"

Great, now the tears were going to start in earnest. She really could use some emotionally stress-free days. Were two in a row too much to ask for? She gritted her teeth against the flood of emotion that wanted to burst forth and didn't even bother answering Alyssa for the moment.

Reece took one look at her face and lurched into motion. "Hey kiddo, I'll tell you what. If it doesn't work out today, I'll give you a ride one of these days when I can work it out with your mom, okay? Right now let's just get your mom fixed up." He unlocked the door and held it until Alyssa could climb inside. "Do you need help buckling up?" he questioned her daughter.

Alyssa's lip was extended in a full pout. "No. I can do it myself."

"Gotcha." Reece shut the door and turned to face Marie. "I'm really sorry. I wasn't thinking what a spot that would put you in. I'll be more careful in the future."

In the future? Marie swallowed. She tipped him a nod of forgiveness.

He opened her door and she sank into her seat while he trotted around to the driver's side.

To her chagrin, she found that while her three-year-old hadn't needed help with her seatbelt, she did. There was no way to keep the compression on her finger and pull the belt across her at the same time. In frustration she gave up. She could just ride to the hospital without one on.

But before she knew what he planned, Reece propped one arm behind her seat and leaned across her to grab her seatbelt. For one split moment he paused and met her gaze, his face, shaded by the brim of his hat, only inches from hers. She smelled the crisp familiar scent of his aftershave and saw the glint of something inviting in his eyes. And then he eased back and clicked her belt in. He adjusted the driver's seat to give more room for his legs and turned the key.

Her car coughed a couple times but didn't catch right away.

"It always does that. You have to pump the gas a little." She tipped her head against the seat rest.

Reece pushed twice on the gas pedal and tried again.

Nothing.

Marie bit the inside of her lip. This was not happening to her, was it? She totally had no money to spend on her car. This day threatened to overwhelm her. She lolled her head over to look at the ocean across the road from Thrift and Save. It stretched into the distance, blue-green meeting blue-gray sky on the sill of the horizon. She pressed her lips together and scrunched her eyes shut. She was not going to cry. That would not solve a single thing.

Reece engaged the starter several more times between pumps, all to no avail. He cleared his throat and glanced over at Marie.

Head back, she was staring out over the Pacific, and he could see the distinct shimmer of extra moisture in her eyes. He wanted to reach over and clasp her shoulder, but shoved his hands under his legs instead. He needed to remember why he'd walked away from her in the first place. He didn't know if she was any closer to the Lord now than she'd been, and no matter how beautiful she was, or how many emotions this woman could make him feel, one thing he did know was that he wanted a marriage where both he and his wife would put God first. That clearly hadn't been the case with Marie the last time they'd been dating.

He shook off the memories. He really needed to get her in to have that finger fixed. "Let me grab my truck and give us a jump. Sit tight. Shouldn't take more than a minute."

He had to park behind her because there were no empty spaces nearby, but thankfully he had long enough cables. He parked, hooked up the cables, and tried the key again. Her little car still wouldn't start.

Marie looked weary.

He did squeeze her shoulder this time, but

only in a gesture of friendship. “One thing at a time, huh? My truck to the hospital and then I’ll help you figure out what to do about your car.”

She sighed softly. “Thanks.”

“My pleasure.” He clicked her seatbelt open and then got out and unhooked the cables and jogged them back to his truck. By the time he came back to grab Alyssa, Marie had already wrestled open the back door. “I’ll get her.” The tyke was sound asleep, a little bunny he hadn’t noticed before tucked under one arm.

Marie moved out of his way, smiling softly. “Can you lift both her and the seat at the same time? We can just leave her belted in and transfer her to your truck.

He grinned at the thought of her questioning whether he could lift a kid, who couldn’t weigh twenty-five pounds soaking wet, and a car seat, which weighed maybe ten. The guys at Deschutes Rejuvenation would get a kick out of that. “Yeah, I think I can manage.”

It didn’t take him long to get both of them buckled into his truck.

As he put the truck in reverse, Marie spoke. “Thanks for taking me. I’m sorry we’re going to end up taking up such a chunk of your day.”

He shook his head and eased the truck out onto the main road. “It’s not a problem, really.” A comfortable silence settled, but he really wanted to know a little more about her life. “So tell me about yourself.”

His peripheral vision caught the lift of one slender shoulder. "Oh you know. Pretty much the same as before, except I have a little girl now."

Disappointment settled.

"I still work at Mom's Gym with Taysia Sumner. Still live in the same apartment. What about you? Where have you been for the past several years?"

The hospital lay just ahead to the right. He put on his blinker and pulled into the lot, parking near the emergency room. "For the past several years I've been working for a wilderness camp for trouble teen boys. They come to us from all sorts of backgrounds and live with us for six months. Hopefully they go home changed. I've loved it. But after eight rotations, I was feeling a little burnout. And then Dad took sick. So..." he shrugged, "I'm here to help mom with the bed and breakfast for the foreseeable future."

"Oh."

Curiosity furrowed his brow as he stopped in a parking spot. Was that disappointment he heard in her tone? He glanced back at Alyssa. "Do you want me to take her out of her seat or just bring her seat in?"

Marie pressed her lips together. "If you don't mind holding her, I think she'll stay asleep longer than if we leave her in the seat."

"I don't mind at all." Carefully, he unbuckled the tyke and lifted her so her head lolled against his shoulder. Locking the truck, he shoved the keys into his pocket and then pressed a hand to Marie's back, directing her toward the emergency entrance.

Her feet seemed to drag until she finally came to a complete stand still. "Do you think I really need stitches?"

"Yes, I'm afraid you will. Listen, if it's the procedure that has you worried, I'll stay with you the whole time."

"No, it's not that. It's just—" She tucked one side of her lower lip between her teeth. "Never mind, let's just get this over with."

Chapter 3

Marie couldn't believe she'd almost blurted out that her finances were already stretched so thin she could read a book through them. Being around Reece was dangerous. He had a way of extracting things from her without her even knowing he was doing it.

The doors to the emergency room whooshed open, and the interior of the money-sucking facility loomed.

Okay Lord, here we go. I could really use some help here. I'm sure You were looking over my shoulder when I was balancing my checkbook the other day? She paused. Why was it she never seemed to turn to God with her concerns before she worried and agonized about them till she was nearly a blubbering puddle? She winced a glance upward. *Forgive me? You are probably wishing I would learn to quit fretting about You providing so You could move on to some other lesson, huh? If I quit stressing will You drop a big check from the sky?* She wrinkled her nose as they stopped before an unoccupied desk behind which a door stood ajar. *Probably doesn't work like that, huh? I know. Okay, I'm trying to let this go. I trust You, I really do. And I'm so thankful for all the ways You've changed me. Help me to keep growing and learning to trust more.*

Reece wore a worried frown. "Are you okay?"

She nodded. "Yep. Just praying a little."

He looked like he wanted to respond to that, but just then a woman in blue scrubs bustled through the door and plopped into the chair behind the desk. She took in Reece and Alyssa first and then her focus zoned in on Marie's bloody shirt. One eyebrow quirked. "What can we do for you today."

Marie lifted the offending appendage still clamped carefully in her other fist. "I cut my finger."

The nurse was already pulling up a form on her computer. "I can see that. How did you cut it and how deep did it look?"

"Uh...on a broken pickle jar, and I think it's pretty deep."

"How much pain are you in on a scale of one to ten? Ten being the most pain you've ever felt in your life."

Marie scrunched up her face. Did it matter if she wasn't in too much pain but might bleed a bucket on their floor? "Two, maybe three?"

The questions continued...and continued.

Marie found a moment to be thankful Alyssa was sound asleep and that Reece was standing by so patiently and even digging out her insurance card for her when he really should be home with his groceries already. And then the dreaded words that she'd known were coming.

"Your co pay is seventy-five dollars. How would you like to pay for that today?"

Marie swallowed. It might as well be a thousand. She would just have to put it on the credit card she'd been trying to pay off. It still carried a good percentage of the medical costs she'd incurred when Alyssa was born a couple weeks prematurely and had needed to stay extra days in the neonatal unit. And the percentage rate was outrageous, but she didn't have any other options.

She glanced apologetically at Reece. "Could you grab the Visa card in my wallet? It has an Oregon Duck logo on it."

Reece gave her an exaggerated wince as he angled his body so Alyssa would stay on his shoulder and dug into her purse for the third time that day. "The Ducks? Everyone knows OSU is the better school." He winked.

A tremor of awareness shot through her. She really needed to put the brakes on her disobedient emotions. She'd barely thought of Dan since she'd heard Reece's voice in the store, and then only because Alyssa had brought him up. Guilt niggled at her. After all, she'd promised the man she would think about his proposal.

Reece was eyeing her as though he expected a response.

She swallowed and shrugged. "The duck was cuter." And would have been the school of her choice if she hadn't gotten pregnant her senior year of high school.

Reece fumbled with something but then seemed to recover, and after a moment he handed the nurse the card.

"Alright, we'll just get you to sign the slip after we can get that finger stitched up for you. Right this way, please."

Thirty minutes later, they were on their way out of the hospital parking lot, Marie with a numb finger that had required seven stitches and a prescription for antibiotics that she probably shouldn't spend money on. Thankfully, they'd said she only nicked the tendon and it should heal up on its own.

It was only 1PM but she was exhausted, and there really wasn't anything at the grocery store they couldn't live without until tomorrow. Besides that, if she didn't get away from this man's kind thoughtfulness real soon she was going to forget she was as contented as a sea gull at a picnic with her life just the way it was. Which was one of the reasons she'd been putting Dan off for a while now. "Reece, if you don't mind, could you just drop us at my apartment? I don't really need the groceries until tomorrow. I'll just go back and make another run at it after church."

He angled her a quick look, then returned his focus to the road. There was a bit of puzzlement on his face, but he only resettled his hat and said, "What about your prescription?"

She waved a hand and tried to come up with something that wouldn't be an outright lie. "Alyssa can finish her nap at home. And we live close to the pharmacy."

"Okay. Not a problem."

"Thanks. Just turn right on Coral. And I'm only a block down on the right."

"So...church? You still attend with Taysia?" Reece's thumbs tapped out a rhythm on the steering wheel.

"Oh, yeah, we all still go together."

"They picking you up?"

She frowned. "No. Why would they— Oh! My car!" She felt the burn of humiliation. He must think she was such a ditz. "Normally I drive Alyssa and me. But I'm sure they won't mind picking us up tomorrow. I'll just give them a call." What was she going to do about the betrayal of her Corolla? She pushed the thought aside. That was a problem for another day.

He cleared his throat and turned on his blinker as Coral approached. "I can pick you up, if you like."

Hadn't she just been telling herself she needed to escape the man's kindness? Yet, it would be easier just to have him get them. And she couldn't just skip tomorrow, because she was on for treats. Maybe she should call Dan and have him get them? But he lived on the other side of the church from them.

She niggled her lip in indecision for a moment before finally saying, "I guess if you don't mind, that would be a big help. Thank you."

"Happy to help."

Her pulse launched into a flat out sprint, and she clenched her teeth in chagrin. He was only offering as a friend. And besides, if it was an offer of more, her answer would be a firm "no." This was the man who had shredded her heart with the efficiency of a meat grinder. What was she thinking, accepting his help?

She wasn't. That's what. It was her exhaustion doing the thinking for her. She would just have to be doubly on her guard, that was all.

Reece eased to a stop in the space in front of her building.

So he'd remembered where she lived.

He hopped out and jogged around to her side to get Alyssa. "I'll get her for you."

Since she didn't know how she would have managed Alyssa and the big car seat with her finger that resembled a mini banana, she only stepped back and thanked him. "I'll get the car seat."

When they stepped into her living room from the breezeway, Reece paused and looked around.

As Marie set the car seat into the small coat

closet where it would be out of the way for the moment, she scanned her apartment.

Her face heated for the umpteenth time that day.

She'd never had a lot of money, and her tastes tended toward shabby chic. She'd repurposed an old straight wooden ladder, painted white and distressed, into a bookshelf along one wall. Several of Alyssa's books lay in a catawampus heap toward one end. An old window-paneled door, that she'd converted into a mirror with coat hooks along the bottom, hung just below that. Even though she liked the scuffed paint look she'd given the piece, Reece probably only saw scratched up junk as he hooked his Stetson on one of the hooks.

The two white wicker chairs were cushioned with pillows she'd made from old jeans – she'd found both the chairs and the jeans at a garage sale and been hit with the inspiration for the project. And the loveseat had come from Goodwill. One of the cushions had been torn, but she'd duct taped it closed and then sewn a couch cover from white flat sheets. Two more of the jean pillows lay on the floor near the TV. Alyssa must have forgotten to put them back this morning before they left for the store.

Marie hurried to pick them up. "Uh...Alyssa's room is just through here." She tossed the pillows onto the couch and hustled down the hall, pushing open the door to Alyssa's room and kicking aside stuffed animals in a path to the bed. She pulled back the blankets.

Reece gently deposited Alyssa against her pillow and stepped back.

Since it was such a warm day, Marie just pulled the sheet up over Alyssa and then turned for the hallway. But Reece hadn't backed away more than a couple steps, and she almost barreled into him. She sucked in a gasp of surprise. But he didn't seem to take notice. His attention roamed the room taking in the eclectic array of crackled pink decor.

Marie pressed her lips together. The only thing she'd actually spent any real money on in this room was the mattress her daughter slept on. Everything else from the dresser to the headboard had either been a gift or ten dollars or less at garage sales or thrift shops. Even the paint in browns and pinks that she'd used to paint and then distress the bed and dresser had been in a free pile at a garage sale. She couldn't tell by Reece's expression whether he liked the look or not.

And oh, why did she care whether he liked it in the first place? Marie cleared her throat.

That seemed to jolt him into action, and he led the way back to the living room.

He unhooked his Stetson and fingered the brim, his gaze roaming the room once more before pausing on her.

She rested her hands on the back of one of the

wicker chairs and tried not to let her fingers fidget with one of the shaggy seams on the denim pillow. To no avail.

Reece's gaze softened, and then warmed, and then twinkled. "It's really nice to see you again."

Drat her misbehaving heart. She swallowed. And instead of saying it was nice to see him too and shooing him out the door like she should, her mouth opened and offered, "I'm sorry to hear about your dad. Let me know if there's any way I can help."

He tapped the brim of his hat against his Levi-clad thigh, his gaze boring into hers. "You're different."

Heat bloomed in her cheeks. So he'd noticed. That ought to give her some measure of comfort. She dipped her chin in a nod.

She really had changed since he'd last seen her. Gone was the nurture-starved girl-woman who'd been looking for love in all the wrong places. Offering her body to – even throwing herself at – any man who would have her (or wouldn't have her, in the case of Reece), in hopes of fulfilling the craving, the gaping need, the itch nothing seemed to be able to scratch. "I finally found the love I'd been searching for in all the wrong ways."

He tapped the hat against his leg again, and a furrow formed between his brows. "This Jackson guy?"

A laugh popped loose before she could stop it.

She scooped a hand back through her hair. "No. I meant Jesus." Come to think of it, she really owed the man an apology. She glanced down and didn't even try to stop herself from fiddling this time. "Reece, I really owe you an apology. That night when I...when I..." She clenched her eyes shut.

Visions of her younger self pressing her body hard against his as they lay on the warm beach sand at dusk. Of her fingers undoing the buttons of his shirt and gliding over the firm warmth of his torso as she kissed him passionately—

Stop. "Reece, I'm very ashamed of many things and that night with you is one of them. I hope you can forgive me. I'm trying to learn to lean on Jesus' forgiveness and learning to forgive myself. And I want you to know I totally understand now why you broke things off the way you did. I must have...repulsed you."

He chuckled, low and raspy.

Her gaze flew to his.

"You remember the story of Joseph and Potiphar's wife, Marie?"

He was changing the subject? She frowned but gave a little nod.

"I can tell you from personal experience that he ran because he was tempted as all get out to give in." With that, he tipped his hat back onto his head, lifted his chin to peer at her from under the brim, and then offered a wink just before he opened the door. "I'll be by at nine thirty to pick you up." Her door clicked shut behind him.

Marie's legs gave out, and she sank to her knees on the floor.

Her thoughts returned for just a moment to that night so many years ago. The night Reece had left his shirt in her hand and quite literally ran to his car and left her in the sand alone. He'd texted her the next day that he couldn't see her anymore and had been only distantly friendly to her every time she'd seen him after that. Every time until this one.

Oh boy. She scooped the fingers of her good hand through her hair. This day was not going as she'd planned.

www.ingramcontent.com/pod-product-compliance
Lightning Source LLC
LaVergne TN
LVHW091036080826
845145LV00002B/518

* 9 7 8 1 9 4 2 9 8 2 5 4 8 *